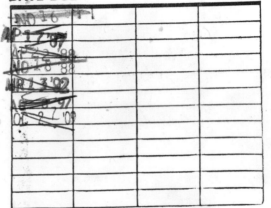

THE RETURN
OF THE
WHISTLER

By Blossom Elfman

THE RETURN
OF THE
WHISTLER

Blossom Elfman

Houghton Mifflin Company

Boston 1981

Library of Congress Cataloging in Publication Data

Elfman, Blossom.
    The Return of the Whistler.

    I. Title.
PS3555.L39R4   813'.54   80-27681
ISBN 0-395-29464-9

Printed in the United States of America

D 10 9 8 7 6 5 4 3 2 1

Some of the characters and parts of this plot are entirely
fictional and bear no resemblance to persons living or dead,
or events that happened. I am not entirely certain, however,
which characters and what incidents. I do assure you that
Barry and Mars and their story are pure fiction. But Beulah
did live and was as I have described. Bits of Arnie and
Mathilda and Red and Arthur existed in various other
people. Part of Patterson and part of Barbara Baker are
myself. And I once taught a remedial class that had a whistler.

For Lillian

With special thanks to Matthew Bright and
Brad Kay, and to Dr. HH, master of triviology.

THE RETURN OF THE WHISTLER

I

Uneasy Riders

SOMETIMES SHE WAS DRIVEN to school in her mother's white chauffeur-driven Caddy. Or she drove in with Barry, in his father's old Porsche with the license that read DACCORD. Arnie might just see her in the other lane, languid cheek resting against the window, all that wheat-colored hair, breasts that swelled over the bindings of her low blouse, warm and soft and movable, like pudding. If she saw him, she rose out of her lethargy and pursed her lips into a kiss. Sometimes. So as they turned off the Pacific Coast Highway and drove up Sunset into the Palisades, Arnie hung close to the window and counted chauffeur-driven cars.

He got one Rolls before the hill crested and one classic Bentley at the top. Traffic backed up and they stopped. So he looked at license plates for a while. The plate on a black Lotus read LAYDBAK. He tried to sound it out, but it didn't mean anything. "Lady-bake. What's lady-bake?"

"You nerd," said Hal. "That's laid-back." Hal sitting up front with his father, dressed like his father, two of those soft

English sweaters, the same necks, the same hair, little swirls at the crown. Hal twisted around to give him a long, sour once-over and said *nerd* again, half-swallowed, between clenched teeth, but audible.

The window was down and Arnie rested his head against the frame, looking out.

Amy jabbed at him with an elbow. "Defend yourself!"

"For what?" He considered the flight of clouds as they moved westward toward the sea.

"You heard what he said!"

"I didn't."

She bounced forward. "Daddy, did you hear him?" She punched Hal hard on the arm.

Hal sank lower in his seat. "Well look at the way he's dressed. He promised me he would wear socks at least."

Arnie dragged up one skinny leg and showed Hal. He was wearing socks. Old grayish-whitish bagged-out-at-the-top cotton tennis socks, and his Tijuana sandals with the bottoms made out of old tires, and his Hawaiian print shirt, rescued from a thousand perils at the hands of several maids in a rather rumpled condition, and his softest jeans with the patch flapping.

"Then will you at least keep a low profile?" said Hal. "Is that asking too much? Just to stay away from the bums?"

Arnie tested a scab on his arm to see if it was ripe for picking. "They're not bums, they're my friends."

Traffic moved forward, they turned a corner, and the blue scrap of sea disappeared.

When they stopped in front of the school, his father kept the motor idling. Hal got out first. He adjusted his shoulders and the collar of his shirt and the bottom edge of his sweater before casually glancing around to see who was watching. Hal was a very handsome guy.

Arnie unfolded himself and got out. He was taller than Hal, even though Hal was older. Hal cast him a final semi-wincing glance. "Do you know how bloody rotten you look?"

Amy bounced out. She was barely five feet tall. She looked and moved like a little Russian gymnast and when she couldn't get satisfaction, she punched. So she punched Hal's arm again. "Two weeks in London and it's *bloody* this and *bloody* that. You're such a put-on!"

"Why don't you stuff it?" said Hal. He hailed a friend and walked through the gate.

The Mercedes was still idling at the curb, so his father wasn't done with him yet. Arnie moved to where he could see a piece of the ocean between high eucalyptus trees. The morning fog was burning off, like gauze peeled away from the sky, layer by layer. *"Arnie!"* He hit his head a hard crack on the window as he leaned in. That crack reflected in his father's face.

"Are you hurt?"

"I'm not."

"You have to anticipate," said his father. "It's very important to anticipate."

"I will."

"You understand why I'm not mixing in between you and Hal."

He did.

"Are you sure, Arnie?"

"I am."

"Amy is only fifteen and I'm not worried about her. Do you know why? Because Amy speaks up for herself."

"I know."

"If you don't speak up for yourself, nobody will."

"Okay."

His father was trying to work something else up, framing the words, pulling his lips back against his teeth as if in pain, the way he did when he was planning something hard for a day in court. Finally he gave up. "Arnie, we're a family. We love each other."

"I do."

"Then give Hal a break."

He waited to find out what kind of break. But his father was finished; he put the car in gear, he waited until Arnie anticipated and carefully withdrew his head, and then drove off.

Amy hugged at his arm for a while. "I put the English answers in the front of your notebook—but copy them in your own writing." He was afraid she was going to reach up and kiss him, but she only slicked at his hair. "I'll eat lunch in the cafe if you need me, and Arnie . . ."

He waited.

"Please don't get into trouble. You know what Daddy said."

Finally she left him also.

Finally.

He let his shoulders slump comfortably and he breathed in the fresh sea air. He sniffed, to see what kind of smells the morning held. Then he reached into his back pocket and touched cold hard metal. It comforted his fingers. From behind the smooth metal he pulled out a folded felt hat and jammed it on his head. The edges of his straw-yellow hair stuck out. He sat down on a huge rock that was part of the landscaping. He bent over to see the bits of ancient sea animals calcified in the pockholes of the rock. He kicked off his sandals and pulled off his socks. He rolled the socks into a ball and tossed them toward a trash can. He missed. Then he put his face up to the sun to get reacquainted with the universe. He wriggled his toes to stir up the crustiness. His two middle toes were longer than the rest. He thought about that for a while. Then he pulled on his sandals and ran a finger over the soft material of his hat and waited until the bus with the black kids from southwest L.A. pulled up.

Arthur Washington wore a Civil War cap, patent leather shoes with pointed toes, very tight black pants, and a vest over a tee shirt. Arthur was six-three, two-twenty. He carried a notebook and a jar that was covered with a cloth and secured with a rubber band. He waved to Arnie. He came

4

over and put a massive arm around Arnie's shoulders. "This the day, man?"

Arnie felt the cool pleasure of that squeeze. He tried to answer something but his feelings were like clouds: they moved and shifted and took shapes but never quite coalesced into anything concrete that he could express. He just nodded.

He and Arthur walked through the gate. A number of people stepped aside or looked at the jar. Arthur kept a black tarantula in that jar. The tarantula's name was Beulah. Nobody knew, except for Arnie and a few, that Beulah was actually a very fuzzy, quite friendly spider. Beulah knew Arthur and loved it when Arthur rubbed her head with the tip of his finger. She had eight eyes, four of which could light up in the dark. She could rear up on her back legs and make a sort of humming sound. Arthur was trying to teach her to talk in signals.

Mathilda and Barry were there already, waiting on a bench. She smiled and pursed him a kiss. Those breasts rose and fell, yeasty and satin, inducing hungers. Barry was Mars Fletcher's son. He had a ferret face. His skin was terrible, either threatening to break out in a virulent pox or subsided into new pits like an expanding map that changed with each new exploration. He wore a slouched explorer's hat that his father wore on location in Africa for the picture that had won an Academy Award. When Barry sat back deep in thought, his eyes slitted, almost Oriental. When he was thinking, he picked at his face. He was picking at it now. "You ready?"

Arnie pulled back his shoulders, his eyes on Mathilda. He nodded. He was.

"Think we can pull it off?"

"I think." Arnie reached back and let his fingers slide over metal, for luck.

Barry rubbed his fist into an open palm. His father always did that. It was a sort of Fletcher trademark. "So we pull it off at the beginning of the hour. *D'accord?*" *D'accord* was

French for okay. Mars Fletcher always said *D'accord*. The license plates of all his Porsches always read DACCORD. Barry had been to Cannes with his father. It was the most important event of his life. "If this works, if we pull this off, the party is on."

Mathilda rubbed her soft self against him. "And Arnie knows what I promised."

His face flushed hot.

"I love you," said Mathilda, purring against him. "And how many people do I love in this world?"

"Hey!" Red hailed them as he moved between trash barrels, twisting his body like a slalom racer. He waved at them with long-fingernailed hands. Red was the master cheat of the universe. He could cheat through anything. He could put answers inside his nails, or scratched into chocolate bars, which he ate after a test. He had a child's face, innocent, like an altar boy. When he protested, he could shed real tears. His hair was carrot and his face white and uncolored by the sun. He slid onto the bench next to Barry. "All set."

"When did you see Llewelyn?"

"Just now."

"What did you tell him?"

"That I only came to him because my father was going to sue the school and I didn't want all that trouble. That Patterson hit me twice. And that once he put a hand on my knee." Red took a derby out of his knapsack and smoothed it lovingly with the back of his sleeve. "I told him, look into the room once, you'll see. And I told him that my father was getting very nervous about it."

Red's father was financial adviser to somebody in the Mafia. Mathilda's mother owned a football team in Texas. Arthur's father was a surgeon in Baldwin Hills, which is the black Beverly Hills. They had a white maid.

And they all hated Averill Patterson. Patterson taught the only remedial English at Pacific West, which boasted the highest academic rating in the city. "Remedial" was the dumping place for all problems that were driving the other finely honed teachers crazy: balky readers, hotheads, impossible cases, and total misfits. It was a penalty course. It usually went by default to the man with the best program. Patterson also taught the elite Victorian Lit. The remedials were Patterson's pariahs. *They* were the penalty. *They* were the dregs. And they knew it. So they hated him and wanted him dead.

Arthur shoved the jar in front of Arnie's nose. "You want to touch Beulah for luck, man?"

Arnie was filled with the brotherhood of the moment. He nodded *yes*. Arthur removed the rubber band and lifted the cloth from the jar. At the bottom of the jar was a little paper sack where Beulah made her nest. She was about four inches across and very hairy. She waved a fuzzy leg into the free air. "Come on out, sweet baby." Beulah walked on long dainty legs into Arthur's hand, pausing to take the sun. A small circle of watchers gathered. Arnie held out a bare arm. Beulah sat for a moment, getting the picture of what was expected of her. She was a super-trained tarantula, very bright for her species. Slowly she walked onto Arnie's arm.

The bell rang for first period. Arnie was still standing with the silly happy smile on his face and Beulah on his arm.

From between the watchers, he saw Hal glowering at him. Hal's face, full of anger, his lips silently moving to shape the word *nerd*.

2

Tell Me Not in Mournful Numbers

THEY WALKED shoulder to shoulder, like a special brigade, the four in their hats and Mathilda. Pacific was a highly civilized school. Usually people stepped out of their way. As they walked along they passed De Haven, who taught the only dumbbell math at Pacific. They had nothing against De Haven, an unmarried lady with a flat chest, who seemed to be drying out from the inside, puckering inward. She didn't greet them, except with a cold stare. But Mathilda broke from the group and ran over to De Haven and took her arm as if they were personal friends. "Listen, I can't come to math today. I have a dentist appointment."

De Haven kept right on walking. "Show me your excuse."

"It's in my locker," said Mathilda.

"Then go to your locker and get it."

"Oh, I think I left it at home," said Mathilda.

"Then I will see you in math," said De Haven.

"But he just put in a temporary crown! It's coming loose!"

"Hold it in with your tongue," said De Haven. "I'll see you in class."

Now Mathilda let go of her arm and just walked beside her. "I only *said* that because I have a much more personal reason, okay?"

De Haven never missed a step. She took her little appointment book out of her purse and checked through her calendar. She smiled and put it away. "Don't forget your textbook," she said.

Mathilda fell behind. She mouthed *bitch* soundlessly.

She fell in step again and took Arnie's arm. As they passed the open door of the math building, the little laughing, talking group of freshmen looked up and saw them. Amy was in that group. Her smiling, bouncy face changed to consternation. Arnie tugged at Mathilda's arm to hurry her. But she only slowed. She leaned over and kissed Arnie's cheek. "Sister's boy," she said.

He felt his face flush hot. "I'm not."

She held tightly to his arm. "It only makes you sweeter."

3

Little Murders

"TIMING," SAID BARRY. "Timing is everything." Barry had pushed just enough of his hat off his eyes so that he could focus on Patterson. "You watch, you wait, you take the moment." Mars Fletcher always said that. It was quoted in all the movie magazines, with the picture of tall, rangy, identifiable Mars slumped in his director's chair, watching and waiting and ready to take the moment. Barry had been watching Patterson for a long time, psyching him out. The moment was now.

He held them back while the rest of the class went in. There were about eighteen in the class. Genuine slows, docile and apathetic. The sports bums, tall, angry, handsome guys who usually sat dreaming of curls of green water or white ski slopes, their feet in the aisles and their eyes on the window. And them. Barry motioned for them to wait, like the starter for a race. Then he snapped his fingers. "Now." Slowly the five of them entered.

Patterson had their hour meticulously organized. It was the only way he survived. On each desk was a little easy-to-read pamphlet, usually about a ghetto or a teenage pregnancy and answer sheets with little fill-in blanks. If he could get them into their seats, if he walked the aisles to keep them from rising or communicating with each other, he could make it through the hour.

They all knew Patterson. They all saw the book of poetry or the pale leather binding of his Shakespeare overturned and open on his desk, how his eyes hungered for that book, how his eyes watched the clock, pained at its slow motion, how he moved among them like a runner doing the gauntlet, fast so as not to be too badly hurt. These pamphlets, these little answer blanks; it was all beneath him. They were a symbol of his defeat. That's why they hated him and wanted him dead. And he knew that. He was a sandy-haired man with a fair complexion. As he looked at them, his pressure rose. If things were really bad, his face would flush red and a white spot would appear on his cheek, like the mark of the devil, or a watermark of warning.

Red greeted him first. "Hi," he said, really friendly, concerned. "You been to the beach or what? Boy, do you have a sunburn."

The red face burned redder. "Sit down," said Patterson. "Take a seat, please."

"How you doin'?" asked Arthur. He bent over Patterson and stared at the face. "Man, you sure got one red face. How come you got such a red face?"

Patterson swallowed hard. He looked at the jar but said nothing. He was really afraid of Arthur's size and color.

"Please sit down."

"Man . . . " Arthur shook his head in sympathy.

"Can I touch it once?" asked Mathilda. "It leaves such funny white spots. What causes that? Did you ask a doctor? I don't want to be near anything contagious."

Arnie walked in quietly, as usual. He smiled at Patterson. He said, "Hi."

Patterson's hand went to his throat and touched it lightly.

They knew the sign. He was checking his pulse.

The bell rang. They took their seats.

It all happened fast. Patterson quickly filled in the absence list. The messenger from the office knocked and stepped in to pick it up. Red rushed to the front of the room, a paper in his hand, as if to ask a question. He was faster than Patterson. He grabbed the list. "I'll take it." As if he were doing Patterson a favor. He carried the list to the door. This caught Patterson off guard. The list was given over, the door closed. Patterson's eyes rested on the desk. The wooden paddle that was the hall pass was missing. When Red returned he had a guilty look and his hands covered something under his teeshirt.

"The pass!" said Patterson in alarm. "Give it to me!"

"Give you what?" asked Red.

"Put the pass back on my desk, please!"

Tears formed in the corners of Red's eyes. "I don't have the pass!"

Patterson's face reddened. The white spot appeared. "You're holding it under your shirt!"

Red appealed for justice. He lifted the shirt. His skin was white, his ribs showed, he looked like a larva newly hatched or something taken unfinished from its source. There was no paddle. Red must have handed the paddle to the office messenger. It might well be in somebody else's hands by now. Patterson rushed out of the room.

Red reached behind him and took the paddle out of his pocket and laid it on the desk. Nobody said a word.

Patterson came back breathing hard. He had to sit down to catch his wind. That was a serious mistake. He saw the pass on his desk. He heard them snicker. They all knew that he had falsely accused the office messenger. You could see the pulse beating in his throat and in his temple. They sat there quietly watching him.

Barry's finger flicked.

Suddenly all chairs scraped, a paper clip flew over Patterson's head, a wet wad of paper hit the board, all books fell.

"Stop this!" Patterson started to walk the aisles as he always did, trying to keep the lid on. Now he stalked, breathing hard, getting out of control. "Why?" He bent to look at faces. "I try to be fair! Just tell me what I've done!"

It was an embarrassment. They bent over desks, fiddled with pencils. They expected a good fight. He had weakened too soon.

He stopped walking. He returned to his desk, really upset. He wanted to be left alone, to read his book of poetry, but he knew that they hadn't given up yet, that this was the eye of the hurricane.

Then the whistle came. A small whistle, a barely perceptible whistle. From over on the right. Patterson turned his head. His face twisted in anger. He tried to see the faces on the right, to identify the whistler. Somebody snickered. Then the whistle came from the left. His head whipped around. No lips moved. Nobody even smiled. The whistle floated low and melodic.

"Stop it," said Patterson lamely.

The whistle came from the front of the room, or seemed to. A small disembodied whistle. A ghost of a whistle. A taunting whistle. Patterson searched face to face. His phantom whistler had returned. His own face got redder. The white spot appeared, like a barometer.

"You have a white spot on your face, Mr. Patterson," said Mathilda. "Why do you have a white spot?"

He tried to do some deep breathing; you could see him pulling air in and out under his palate. His eyes searched the room, the lips, the mouths. As if, if he could only find the source of the whistle he would solve the whole puzzle of why he, who had once taught Victorian Lit at Swarthmore, should be here with these bums.

Then the quality of the whistle changed, became sharper, less melodic. It came from Red, whose lips were pursed.

Patterson's eyes found him. "So it was you," said Patterson bitterly. "I should have known."

"I swear it wasn't!" Red protested.

"Get out of my room," said Patterson, advancing down the aisle to Red's seat.

"But why?" Red pleaded, his hands upraised in supplication, tears already in his eyes. "I didn't do anything!"

Patterson reached down and pulled Red out of his seat by the front of his shirt. Patterson was a gentle, peaceable soul who never made a wrong action or used a strong word. The books on his desk were *Pippa Passes* by Robert Browning, or "Patterns" by Amy Lowell. He glowered at Red and said, "Get your ass out of my room." He dragged him toward the door.

Barry gave a little finger signal. The whistle floated over Patterson's head, the little musical whistle, the little birdcall. Patterson knew he had been had.

The door opened. Llewelyn stepped in. "He has his hands on me," said Red. "All the time! Ask anybody!"

Patterson, horrified, let go of Red's shirt.

"What did he do?" asked Llewelyn.

The little wings of Patterson's nose flared, like a horse steaming up. You could see the pulse beating in his throat. "He was whistling."

"Oh, come now . . ." said Llewelyn.

Patterson didn't exactly pass out. He asked to be excused. He ran out, trying to catch some air.

Llewelyn dried his brow with a folded linen handkerchief. He looked apologetically at Red. "Tell your father that I most certainly will look into this."

"I know that," said Red, smiling gently. "That's why I came to you."

"Mr. Patterson is unwell," Llewelyn explained to the class. They all made sympathetic noises.

"Do you have something to keep you busy until I can get a sub?"

They bent busily over their papers, assuring him.

Llewelyn left, leaving the door open.

Victory!

Barry stood up, he raised his arms, he began to snap his fingers, he danced in the aisle like Zorba the Greek, doing intricate footwork until he reached the front of the room. He kicked the door shut. Then he danced over to Arnie, took off Arnie's hat, and kissed the top of his head.

Arnie was the whistler. He was the master whistler of the universe. He belonged to the "hatted" ones, the masters and mistresses of deception. Appreciation warmed him from all corners of the room.

Barry took a beatific attitude, making a sign on his breast and then blessing Arnie, like the Pope. "The party is on," said Barry, "and the party is for you."

Mathilda pursed her lips and blew him a kiss. She mouthed *I love you.*

It was over.

The class settled in for the rest of the hour. A few of the genuine students bent over papers, or moved their lips to sound things out.

Arnie reached into his back pocket. His fingers touched metal, but it was warm metal now, warm from his body heat. He pulled it out and held it in the palm of his hand. It was a Hohner, a mouth organ, a harmonica. He cupped it sensuously, familiarly. He shoved his hat down, half over his eyes. He began to play, softly, hardly louder than the whistle, but with much passion. He played out how he felt that morning when Hal turned around and looked at him in the car, he played the kind of alarm he always felt with the approaching day, he played his warm night dreams. He played all that. Then he played the softness of his desires, Mathilda's breasts, something about clouds, sucking into the Hohner, fanning it for texture. The music veiled the room with magic.

He was still playing when Mrs. Corregian came in to babysit them.

4

Mother Superior

MRS. CORREGIAN TAUGHT Alternative Life Styles, Home Management, and Boys' Cooking, which Barry loved. In fact, she was the only woman in the world he respected. She was a big woman, large bosom, thick waist, she had an accent like Julia Child's, and she brooked no opposition. All she had to do was descend on you, bosom first. Nobody opened a mouth to her.

And she was furious with them. "This was my free hour, you little buggers." Most of them laughed. By sixth period they would be baking brownies in her class, or making quiche. She was big on French cuisine. Which Barry adored. He got the love of cooking from his father.

She pinned her proscriptive gaze on Barry. "What is it with you, Fletcher?"

He leaned back, totally content. "When I was in Cannes, I ate sea urchins from a peddler's cart. They were spiny and wet from the sea. He cut them open with scissors and we just swallowed them raw."

"If somebody opened your head," she said, "they would see a mess of urchins, all right."

It washed right over him. "My father and I had a broccoli quiche at the Orangerie. Can we make a broccoli quiche?"

Arthur had Beulah out for a walk on his desk. He moved two fingers in front of her and she followed him, like a dancer learning a routine. Mrs. Corregian detested spiders. She shuddered when she looked at Beulah. "I wonder if I could do that thing in chocolate sauce the way they do grasshoppers."

Arthur bent protectively over Beulah. "Don't you mind, baby. The lady just don't understand."

She sighed in resignation. She settled her big body in Patterson's chair and opened her recipe books.

Mathilda started to raise her hand. Mrs. Corregian zapped her with a booming command: "Don't you dare!"

Mathilda quickly put down her hand.

Red tucked his shirt into his pants.

Arnie held out his Hohner, waiting permission.

"That poor man." She shook her head in commiseration with Patterson. "He didn't have a chance." But she loved Arnie's music. He always played while the bread was rising. "Go ahead. Play something. Soothe the savages."

They went comfortably back to their fill-in blanks. They knew she liked them. So they were content. About her was the scent of flour and yeast and warm, sugary things. Arnie played quietly until the end of the hour.

They all filed out except Barry, who was still euphoric with success, and Arnie, who was winding down the music. Barry stopped at Mrs. Corregian's desk and gave her a respectful, courtly bow. He took her pudgy great hand and kissed the backs of her fingers.

"Barry," she said, "you would stagger Freud. What is it you're so hungry for?"

Barry flushed. His face was starting to break out again, great red welts that would soon be pustules. He walked out.

Arnie cleaned his Hohner and put it away. As he walked by, Mrs. Corregian caught him by the bottom of his Hawaiian shirt. "Do yourself a favor, Arnold. Change schools."

He wasn't listening to her. He was watching the rear of Mathilda swinging out of the room.

He waited until Mrs. Corregian let go of him, and like an obedient puppy, he followed Mathilda.

5

Where the Wild Things Are

MATHILDA PRESSED HER warm koala-bear body against his arm. "I *know* I promised! And I love you, Arnie. Who else do I love in this world anyhow? The whole world sucks. And you are so precious. You know a lot more than you let on and you're never hurtful. You know how many people are hurtful in this world?"

Her voice had a *but* in it.

"But I have herpes, Arnie. There are about three guys I intend to give herpes to, and one of them is not you. So I got you somebody else for the party. I promised you this was your party and it is. She's dying to meet you."

He felt his heart sinking. The signals were wrong.

She turned her sweet face to his. Her breasts rose and fell, velvet and warm. "Don't you trust me?"

"Yes."

"Would I hurt you?"

"No."

"So I'll bring her over during lunch. Arnie, we are going to make this so nice for you."

He ate lunch by himself. To figure out what he could have misunderstood. He bought a hamburger but it tasted like cardboard. He tossed it and sucked at his chocolate milk with a straw.

Then he saw Mathilda looking over heads for him. He tried to make himself invisible. She was moving toward him with somebody. He got immediately alarmed. Somebody was a kind of wild thing. And then they were making their way through lunchers in his direction. The other one wore the same Jordache jeans but she was chunkier and thicker and the waist was unbuttoned. She wore the same scoop-necked blouse but her boobs were big and womanly. And her hair was crazy—halfway between Bette Midler and the Bride of Frankenstein. He wanted suddenly to find Amy. The other one was arguing with Mathilda but Mathilda had her firmly by the arm. "Here she is, Arnie. This is my best friend, Francesca de la Paula. You know her mother from all those horror movies. Her mother is the one who goes crazy and cuts everyone up. This is her daughter, Francesca. You can call her Francie."

Arnie tried to respond but alarm had thrown him out of commission. He knew he was grinning and he couldn't turn it off.

Francie responded to him the way you respond when you see something awful under a rock. She screwed up her face. She had a slightly bulbous nose and her teeth were silver with braces. "Mathilda, are you *serious?*"

Mathilda put an arm around Arnie's shoulder. "He is supersweet and he's a friend of mine. So take it or leave it, Francie."

Francesca pulled at a wild strand of her hair. She bit at the edge of a cuticle already bitten down to the quick. "Is he a retard or what?"

"I don't want you to talk about my friends that way," said Mathilda. "So what is it? Yes or no?"

He wanted suddenly to cry. He needed Amy.

Francesca screwed up her mouth and pulled at a wiry strand of her electric hair. "Okay," she capitulated, as if it were the worst of all possible choices. Mathilda winked at him, pursed her lips in a kiss, and led the protesting Francesca away.

Arthur moved onto the bench with his hero sandwich. He let Beulah out on his knee. She must have eaten already, pushing away little undigested pieces of things, smoothing herself down tidily.

Arnie wanted desperately to ask something, but he didn't know how to ask it.

Arthur put an arm around him. "Listen man, don't worry about it. It will be dark. And we'll be around."

Barry moved onto the bench, spread a linen napkin on his knees, and opened a jar of oysters. "Believe me, this will be the night of your life. A major production. I never let my friends down."

When he could leave them, Arnie walked across the quad toward the gym, and then out across the field to the hill that cut down from the campus toward the sea. He kicked off his sandals and sat on a bench and took out his Hohner. He rubbed it against his pants to give it polish. He licked at it and cupped it in his hand and held it against his lips and waited for the thing he needed to play.

6

I Am a Rock
I Am an Island

HE WAS SO DEEPLY INTO what he was playing that when
the bench jiggled it shocked him.

"It's okay, it's cool," said Francie. She was sitting on the
end of the bench, her hands jammed into the pockets of her
jeans, the top of her chubby belly hanging over the waistband.

He felt totally violated. He turned his eyes away from her
face and jammed his Hohner into his pocket.

She turned her face up to the sun and pushed back her
wild hair to tan the hidden places. "How did I know you
were a music genius? I should have known that Barry wouldn't
hang around with a retard, okay? So what are you, some kind
of idiot savant or something?"

He froze up.

She grimaced as she spoke, every little word squeezed with
effort out of total boredom. "I said idiot *savant,* dummy! Don't
you understand English?"

He looked for escape.

"I didn't put you down! I just happen to be Mensa, okay?

I have this astronomical IQ, that's all. An idiot savant is somebody who is a genius at one thing and a total zero at everything else."

He kept his eyes on her feet. She wore high heels like Mathilda but her ankles were too thick and the straps cut them. "So if you want to go to Barry's party, I'll go. That's all I wanted to say."

"I'm not going," he said.

She bit at her lower lip. In fact her lower lip looked quite bitten. "I have to go to that party, Arnie. Mars Fletcher is going to show. Barry thinks he might use me in his next picture."

He looked at her silver teeth and at the fleshy nose and the crazy hair. "Why should he?" he asked in candor.

She turned her face sideways to show him. "Impish and unpredictable. Like Liza Minnelli. I saw *Cabaret* fifty times."

If it were funnier, he might have laughed.

"I met her twice. I also knew Paul Newman. I slept with Paul Newman once."

"I don't believe you," he said.

She poked at the end of her nose with a nail-bitten finger. "Don't let the nose bother you. I'm getting it done as soon as it's ripe. So we'll have a good time, okay, Arnie? You take me to the party, I come through for you."

"I'm not going."

She bit at a piece of loose cuticle. "You think I care? I've been turned down by worse nerds than you."

She started back toward the campus. She had fat upper thighs and the rough material of her jeans brushed together making a sound like a grasshopper rubbing its legs.

The fifth-period bell rang. He turned away from the campus and ran.

7

Birds of a Feather

ARNIE RAN THE REST OF THE WAY down the hill and climbed the fence and dropped into freedom. He ran about a half-mile down to the beach. The whole white slope of the sand was empty and cleaned by the wind, rippled and full of birds. He walked the fringes of the ocean, his toes in the white foam.

He sat on the sand and watched the way the water sucked at the rocks and how the cliffs fell away toward the sea. He watched birds from the north in migration. He saw a bird drop out of the sky and land crookedly on the wet sand near him. It surprised him, coming that close. It wasn't a gull. It was bigger, and snowy, with a beak of curved ivory and webbed leathery feet. He could see that the wing was hurt. The bird stretched out the wounded wing, trying to flap it, but it couldn't make it off the ground. Time after time it tried, until finally it folded its wings and sat.

Then he saw the other bird, high in the air, flying its arced circles. It swooped down and squawked at its wounded friend, calling the beached bird back to the sea. But the broken bird couldn't fly. Then the great flying bird dove down and began to scream for its friend to come. And then when it failed at that, it began to peck, with its sharp beak, at its own friend's head! Pecking and pecking until it drew blood and the white feathers were speckled red with it. Arnie ran at the hurt bird, flapping his arms. "Go!" he called. The flying bird took off and circled but swooped back, fanning its own great wings, pecking harder. Arnie had to stand away from the great batting of wings.

Then the pecking bird just gave up. For a while it circled overhead, and then it flew away. "Don't!" cried Arnie. He ran back to the wounded one, shooing it. It flapped wildly, suddenly made it off the ground, but it only landed on an offshore rock and sat there.

For a long while Arnie watched it from the sand, hoping that the other bird would fly back from the sky and land beside its friend and wait for the hurt wing to heal. But the flying bird wasn't coming back. It would never come. And the bird left behind just folded its wings, its head hunched down. Arnie knew that it would be on that rock forever.

8

My Son, My Son

ARABELLE WAS BOILING lobster. Pastry shells stood cooling on the table. Lobster in shells meant company. He opened the refridge to scout. "Who's here?"

She looked up from the pot in dismay. "Where did you get the shirt?"

He smoothed it down with his hand. He took some Jarlsberg cheese and rye bread and some thin-sliced prosciutto and the Dijon mustard.

"I had that shirt in the trash."

"It's my best shirt."

"I should've known better. I should've tore it up for dusting rags."

"Do we have company, or are we just having lobster *per se?*" *Per se* was a joke on his father. Because his father said it in court.

"Your little auntie from Santa Barbara is here. The one with all the gold on her."

"Tante Miriam? How come?"

"I am not invited in participating in the social plans of this house. I don't know how she walks with all that jewelry. In olden days people used to keep all their gold on them in case they got stole by another tribe. But she smells so heavy, nobody would take her."

Miriam was about four-ten, she had tiny feet like the bound feet of Chinese women, she wore high stiletto heels, her hair was upswept and lacquered hard, almost solid. Around her throat she wore pearls and gold chains, on her little wrists bracelets and bangles and gold charms. There were rings on her fingers and she wore an ankle chain. Her lips were painted thickly red and her long nails lacquered, like the figures on the Chinese vases in the living room.

He added some goat's cheese and a hunk of salami and some of the little jar of ordinary caviar. He loved the salt crunch of the eggs.

"Don't spoil your appetite and change your clothes before you come down."

"I'm not coming down. I'm sick."

"Sick like a fox. You in trouble at school again?"

He started toward the stairway with his stuff. Then he saw that the library door was open and he caught a scent of Tante Miriam. She was amusing to watch. He just stopped at the door for a second. She and his mother were having their tea from a little table in front of the soft leather sofa. His mother was always polite but unnerved by Miriam. So she always sat slightly back and away from the scent, like someone leaning into the wind. "I don't want to talk about it," his mother was saying.

"Well, you have to talk about it. I'm not saying it's only your problem. Look at Marshall. Do you think I sleep nights with Marshall?"

His mother stirred her tea, he could hear the little clicking of the spoon against the cup. "What on earth could be wrong with Marshall? Marshall exceeds your expectations."

"A *B* in chemistry?" said Miriam. "There go his chances for a Grade One med school. He stood in a phone booth for a half-hour before he had the heart to call us."

"That's terrible," said his mother with a stony face.

"It was some girl, naturally. Well he got rid of her. He lives in his room now. His nose isn't out of his books. And his father is talking to a few people."

"Talking about what?"

"About what," said Miriam with a little sniff and a touch to the nose of her scented handkerchief. "His father is talking to a few influential people. About the B."

"I see," said his mother coldly. "Then you're not above bending over backwards to help your children. Why are you blaming me?"

"You have three children," said Miriam. "You must think of Hal and Amy. You can't let this foolish guilt blind you."

"I will not discuss it," said his mother.

"You can't keep burying your head and treating him as if he were normal."

He felt suddenly cold. Coldish. He was coming down with something. He felt himself sinking into water greenly. Into slime. And Hal sinking down beside him. No, swimming beside him, his mouth bubbling *nerd, nerd, nerd.*

His nose started to itch.

"He's a slow boy, Beatrice."

"Slow is not abnormal!" his mother flared. "You never make the distinction."

"When did I say abnormal? I only said slow. Very slow."

"Nobody agrees on his index when he's tested. He holds back. You know the way Arnie is, always holding back."

"That is your observation. If he had anything, why would he hold it back?"

"In his own way he has a great deal of talent. He's the musical one in the family. Grant him that."

"A harmonica? A flute, perhaps. Even a flute. If Marshall

turned up a talent on a flute, I'd nip it in the bud. What life can you make on a flute? In fact, the boy can't be trained for anything here at home. And it's depressing for the other children."

He sneezed. His hands were full. He couldn't stifle it. He walked quickly toward the stairs.

Tante Miriam came rushing out into the hall. "My God! Did he hear me?"

He reached the top without spilling. He heard her little machine-gun heels behind him on the steps. He made it to his bedroom and locked the door. His mother knocked insistently. "Arnold, please let me in!"

He didn't answer.

"Arnold?" Tante Miriam tapped with her jangling fingers. "Darling, I only wanted to say hello!"

"It's okay. I'm just tired. I ate already. Ask Arabelle."

He waited until they walked away. His mother screamed at Tante Miriam all the way down the steps.

He changed into his pj's. He hauled out the big encyclopedia his father had given him from where it had sat untouched in his bookcase. Herpes . . . *H* . . . *Her*. . . . He didn't want to think about Mathilda's betrayal. It was probably his fault. He didn't know how. But he never knew and it usually was.

He sat at his desk for a while turning over his polished sea stones. Jades. The speckled browns. His best agate. He checked his aquarium. The angelfish were hiding behind their favorite coral. A couple of clown fish darted in and out of the seaweed. The snub-nosed baby shark came to the glass and looked out at him.

Finally he got into bed with his supplies and turned on the TV. Sometimes he lucked out with cartoons. Once in a while they did the old ones, from the forties. Like the Turkeys, which was played by the Harmonica Rascals. All these crazy turkeys doing country music. Only they didn't play it often. The screen cleared. Just a Tom and Jerry. He clicked to another station. Ah! The Little Skunk! One of his super-favorites! He made himself a sandwich and fluffed up his pillows. Poor little unloved skunk, no girl, nobody who didn't turn a nose up at him. He wants to be popular. So he goes to Acme Costume Rental and rents a Frank Sinatra suit. Now he's tall and gaunt and the girls start screaming when they see him. He sings like Sinatra. Crazy! Everybody loves him now. The girls crowd around him. Especially one girl. He's happy. His heart goes out to her . . . *thump-thump*. But he knows that she's a real girl and he's a skunk in disguise. It's never any use when you're a skunk. He takes off his suit. The game is up. But she doesn't run away. She doesn't turn up her nose in disgust! Suddenly she takes off her own disguise suit. Surprise—she's a skunk also! A beautiful brown-eyed girl skunk! And she loves him!

He clicked off the TV. He cupped the Hohner and began to play. A couple of people knocked. After a while they stopped. He played out the death of Patterson. He played Corregian and her warm rising breads. He played Mathilda's breasts, her softness, his desire. He played Francie, her wild hair. He played out *idiot savant,* two words yoked together like mismatched oxen. He played *herpes.*

He was still playing when his tutor knocked and called his name.

9

A Matter of Degree

M R. SCHECTER ALWAYS SLOUCHED in loaded with books, his heavy shoulders pulled down by the weight, that great thatch of coarse black hair and the hooked nose, like some wild animal moving slowly through a thicket. He raised his head slowly to look at Arnie in bed. He dropped the books on Arnie's desk. Arnie pulled the covers up around him. Mr. Schecter closed the door. He made his usual slow surveillance of the room with his usual sneer. The TV. The remote button on Arnie's bed, near Arnie's fingers. The plate of food. The pajamas. "You got a new TV?"

"It's the downstairs one. Mine broke."

"A little twenty-one-inch color toy."

"It's not a toy," said Arnie.

Mr. Schecter bent to look into the tank. "You got a new shark."

"The last one died."

Mr. Schecter sighed a long *hmmmmmmm*. "How much does a new shark cost?"

He didn't answer.

"A twenty-one-inch color TV? What does it cost?"

He didn't know.

"Where's your notebook? I'm supposed to be broadening your base. Come on, Arnold. Estimate for me what a shark costs. What a TV costs. Round numbers."

"I can't today. I'm coming down with something."

"Can't or won't?" said Mr. Schecter.

He didn't answer.

"So how did your week go?"

Arnie shrugged.

"In words. Phrases. With sound. I'm supposed to be encouraging your elocution. Round syllables, Arnold."

He didn't answer.

"Something. Did you see a movie? Did you watch something exciting on TV?"

"I didn't," he said.

"You have the remote in your hand and you didn't watch."

"I don't remember," he said.

"Let me help you. *Starsky and Hutch*. Did you watch *Starsky and Hutch?*"

"No."

"Did you watch cartoons? *Tom and Jerry? Mighty Mouse?* Watch the old mouse fly through the air and have fantasies of being superboy?"

"No."

"No. He says no."

"I didn't watch *Mighty Mouse.*"

"You didn't do anything. You just lay there in bed with your caviar and your Jarlsberg looking at the ceiling. Or involved in other *unmentionables*. If you did, don't tell me—I don't want to know." He pulled a chair up to the bed. "Justice. Do you understand justice, Arnold?"

"What kind?"

"What kind?" he asked. "The ironic kind. Here is Adam Schecter, Ph.D. Columbia, who cannot get for himself tenure and has to settle for six hours a day in an inner-city school plus twenty-odd dollars an hour teaching children of the idle rich. Children who by dint of simple inheritance can lie slug-abed eating imported caviar . . ."

"It's not imported."

"A matter of *degree,* Arnold. Children who can lie back watching *Sesame Street* without stirring their brains and the earth falls into their laps."

Arnie didn't answer.

"Do you know what Jarlsberg costs a pound?"

He didn't.

"I'm asking you an academic question! Take up your little pencil and write for me how much you estimate Jarlsberg costs a pound. That's what I'm here for. To teach you simple practical sums."

He didn't answer.

"And without lifting a finger you'll inherit. Even though you are a second son. Because Harold the Great, Harold of the Big Mouth who doesn't give the time of day to Adam Schecter who holds a straight A from Columbia grad school, Harold the Prig will probably kick off at forty from a myocardial infarc-tion and Arnold the Silent will inherit . . ."

"What's a myocar——"

". . . while I work off my ass in the bowels of the earth and drag myself here for twenty an hour only to watch you eating caviar and Jarlsberg cheese. Now I ask you, is that justice?"

"I only get eight dollars a week allowance. I'm not rich. I'm not inheriting anything."

"*Only* eight?" His question was directed at some higher forces; he looked up toward the ceiling. "Did you hear that? *Only* eight? Children in India could live a year on eight dol-lars."

"A first-run movie costs five in L.A."

"In Tijuana you see tin-roofed shacks, and children who in their own language are bright and eager, who never get the chance——"

"I didn't stop them," said Arnie.

33

Mr. Schecter started to say something else and then he got angry. His nose reddened. "Open your book and let's get to the reading. Your little sister can do your homework, but she can't read for you, can she?"

"I have a headache."

"I still say you're dyslexic but you have them all fooled, don't you, Arnold. Arnold the Quiet, who will end up with the house and the Mercedes by lying in bed with his caviar and crackers. Are we reading or not?"

"Not."

"Do you want me to leave and pass up the twenty bucks?"

He didn't answer.

"Then keep your book open on your lap."

Arnie opened a book.

"Do you want me to read to you? *This is the best of times, the worst of times?* Will you listen to other men's gems and think about them?"

"Okay," said Arnie.

"Would you prefer Dickens or shall I read you Shakespeare?" The sneer returned and would be there for the rest of the hour. "No, not Shakespeare. You don't understand the metaphor, do you Arnold? As I understand it. Shall I read you *Alice in Wonderland*? Shall we both go into free fall for the rest of the hour? State your preference. It's your twenty, Arnold. You and yours."

"I don't care."

Mr. Schecter read to himself for the rest of the hour. Arnie kept a book open on his lap but he played the Hohner in his head to block out the top of Mr. Schecter's head, that thick brush of hair falling over his eyes as he leaned his round shoulders over the book in his lap.

When the hour was over, his mother knocked and came in. Mr. Schecter smiled up at her and closed his book. He reached over and closed Arnie's book. "Good progress. Very good. I can feel it. Although it would be better I think with three hours rather than one for the week. But . . ."

34

"If you think it's necessary," she said anxiously.

"Good progress. One of these days this boy . . ." He reached over and tousled Arnie's hair. "This boy might find himself applying to Columbia."

"Oh do you think . . ." said his mother with pangs of hope radiating her face.

"Who can predict," said Mr. Schecter. He smiled and ducked a bow and walked out with his books.

His mother hung around for a while waiting for a topic of conversation to open itself up. When it didn't she walked out also.

He went to sleep early.

He dreamed he could talk to animals.

He was disappointed when morning came.

10

The Sound of
One Hand Clapping

ARNIE TRIED TO SLIP OUT of the house but Arabelle caught him. "They have been waiting breakfast for you. So you go in there like a gentleman and eat something." She slicked down his hair. "They are having a big English breakfast for your auntie. Two weeks in London and the whole house is eating kidneys. Kidneys is not human food."

He laughed. "Kidneys" was a joke between Arabelle and him.

"I baked you a few fresh brioches, Arnie, the ones you love, and there is cream cheese. You are too skinny for words."

He saw his father and mother coming down the hall, napkins in hand, looking distraught. He appealed to Arabelle. She turned away. So he figured he was stuck for breakfast.

He could see that his father and mother had already been at it. "Son," said his father apologetically, "you know your Tante Miriam didn't mean anything. You know the way she talks."

"I know."

His mother was livid. His mother played out the counter-melody. In a way it was funny. In a way. "Why are you giving him double messages! Miriam *did* say something! Is he supposed to believe she didn't!"

His father looked nervously toward the dining room. "She'll hear you."

"Then let her! And you let your son know that you feel your sister said a wretched thing."

"It's okay," said Arnie.

"No," she insisted, "it is not okay. Just let somebody say something about her precious Marshall." She came at him with hugs and lugubrious eyes. "I want you to say how you feel, the truth. Tell your father. I'm here to stand behind you."

"Will you stop protecting him every time he gets into trouble? Arnie cut school yesterday. Did you ask him to answer for that? How many times does it make, Arnie?"

His mother kept an arm around his shoulder. "And if he cannot answer! If he cannot!"

"Then he'll have to. He'll damn well have to."

His mother reconsidered what she said. She always reconsidered. Everything she said, she said twice. "I didn't mean *cannot,* I meant Hal doesn't have to answer for every move, so why does Arnie?"

"This is a hard life," his father began. From the kitchen door Arabelle mouthed the old familiar ". . . *hard life, hard life* . . ." He grinned. He wished he hadn't. His father saw it. "I don't need jokes from you, Arnie. You think this is a joke?"

"I don't," he said.

"Why is it hard?" his mother persisted. "How hard is it for Hal, going off to England as a freshman, with all that allowance."

"That's an investment," said his father. "In his future. I have to know that Arnie has a future also."

Now his mother linked an arm in Arnie's. He tried to extricate himself without offending, but it wasn't easy.

"Arnold has to know where he's going." His father looked to him for response.

He didn't know what he was supposed to say. "Where is there to go?"

His father's face reddened. "And I don't need a smart mouth from you." His father returned to the dining room.

His mother smoothed down his hair and kissed him. "Why do you make jokes when it's so serious?"

He wasn't making a joke. And he didn't know why they thought he was. His face probably. He caught a glimpse of his face in the kitchen mirror. And his mother's face. He didn't see how he came from her. But she had her arm linked with his as if he did. He was led into the dining room. Arabelle gave him a commiserating look. He was stuck for breakfast.

The table resettled itself. Amy gave him an eye signal and fanned away the heavy Tante Miriam perfume. Hal was making all the conversation, eating his kidneys with his knife in the right hand and the fork in his English left hand. "Arnold!" called Miriam brightly. "Come and have some breakfast, darling."

Arnie picked up a plate. "How come you're eating with the wrong hand?" he asked Hal. It was a joke on Hal. Only Hal wasn't laughing. He just put down his fork.

Miriam blew him a fragrant kiss. "Darling, guess what I brought you for your birthday."

He took his plate to the sideboard. "It's not my birthday." He came back with a buttered brioche and a mess of Arabelle's eggs. He loved Arabelle's eggs. She made them dry.

"Guess," said Miriam, clinking metal as she moved her little hands.

"Guess about what?" asked Arnie.

Miriam gave his mother a significant glance, and in a lowered voice she said, "He has such a short retention."

"He isn't *deaf*," said Amy. "He can *hear* you, Tante Miriam."

"Don't use that tone at the table," warned her father.

"Well, Miriam made a crack about Arnie and we don't do *that* at the table, do we."

"Arnie is entitled to answer for himself. He knows that." Amy shoved him with her elbow. "De*fend* yourself."

"For what?" asked Arnie.

Tante Miriam gave him one of her little half-pitying smiles, the ones she used for the poor and the indigent. "Arnie knows I love him."

"And you don't have to talk slow," said Amy.

"Montgomery Ward," said Miriam definitively.

He put down his fork.

"Two hundred shares, for your portfolio."

He sat looking at the mound of eggs.

Hal nudged him. "That's very generous, Tante Miriam. Thank Tante Miriam, Arnie." Hal nudged him again, harder.

In the little moment of hesitation, he heard somebody outside the house, leaning on a horn, a long blast. Somebody called, "Ar*nieeee!*"

Everybody turned to the window. Arabelle, drying her hands on her apron, called from the doorway. "There is somebody in a low Italian car calling for Arnie."

He excused himself and walked out. The argument was forming a storm behind him.

Francie was sitting in a purple Maserati. She was wearing purple pants to match the car and a white ruffled blouse that made her look like an overblown flower. She had the car door open for him. "Get in."

"I'm having company breakfast. Don't lean on the horn."

"Just get in the car a minute, *will* you?"

He sat on the edge of the seat with the door open. "What do you want?"

"Okay," she said, getting down to business. "You can drive the Maserati. My mother uses the classic Daimler when she's working, so you can have this car for a week. Two weeks. Whatever."

"I don't have a license."

"Oh my God," she said in total frustration. "Okay, you can have this." She handed him a gold cigarette lighter with the initials DJB. "I can have the initials changed. It's solid gold. Do you know what gold costs an ounce?"

"I don't smoke."

"Then don't use it! Just look at it! It's made in Italy!"

"I don't need a lighter."

She reached back and took a paper sack off the seat and handed it to him. "I had to look all over town. I didn't know whether you were into jazz or the old country stuff. So I got a Toots Thieleman and a De Ford Bailey. The Bailey is a collector's item. It cost me more than fifty bucks."

He turned over the records. He fingered the crisp brown jacket of the De Ford Bailey. "What do I have to do for it?"

"I just want to go to the party, okay?"

"I'm not going." He set the records down on the seat and closed the door and started back toward the house.

But they were all standing at the window, like a painting. Little lacquered Miriam, his hurt mother, Amy looking betrayed, Hal's dark anger.

The car was still parked at the curb. She opened the door for him and he got in. "I figured the records would get you."

"I just need a ride to school. I'm not going to Barry's party."

He closed the door without looking back toward the house. She put the car in the wrong gear and it backed up and hit the base of the big palm. The gears ground painfully. Finally they jolted forward and sped down the hill.

11

Black Holes
and Englishmen

"How can you stand that jock of a brother?" Francie
drove the Maserati about fifty down Sunset, changing lanes,
keeping the heel of her hand ready to the horn. "He makes
me want to puke."

"You mean Hal?"

"How many pukey jock brothers do you have?"

"He's going to college in England."

"England? What for?"

Arnie smiled. "He likes kidneys."

He looked over at her as she drove. Her eyes seemed tired,
red around the edges, as if she hadn't slept. She saw him looking, and she jammed on some purple-rimmed sunglasses. "I
was up part of the night with this Kirlean photography thing."

"What's that?"

"I happen to have a photographic mind. So somebody tells
me something and then I'm stuck with it. Like black holes, for
instance. I stay awake all night with the thing going around in
my head. If your brother goes to Oxford or someplace he'll be
out of your hair. Do you detest him?"

"What's Kirlean photography?" asked Arnie.

"Aura. Everybody has this electric aura. If you take a picture in the dark, you see this wild circle of light that some people emanate. I bet I could photograph your brother Hal and I'd get zero. He has as much personality as a stale banana."

He looked at her frizzed hair, in a halo around her head. He thought of the cartoon where somebody puts his finger into an electric light socket. She was funny. "What's a black hole?"

She changed lanes quite a bit. "Did you know that you could take a human fetus, for instance, and graft it into the uterus of a cow and transport the cow out of the country and then remove the human fetus and put it into the uterus of another woman?"

"Why would anybody want to?"

She stopped for a light but she didn't keep her foot on the brake. She gently rolled into a VW Diesel. The guy at the wheel turned angrily. She backed up and swerved around him, made a U-turn, and sped away in the opposite direction. "That's the whole point. I lie awake half the night dreaming up spy stories, things like that. I'm a triviologist. My whole head is stuffed with that junk."

When she stopped for the next light, the same VW stopped behind her. The guy got out.

Arnie slumped down in his seat trying to be invisible. Francie opened her window wide and leaned out. "Start something!" she shouted. "Go ahead! Hit me!" She leaned out her chin as an easy target.

The guy got a clear look at her, at Arnie, at her hair, at the purple pants. He turned and got back into his car.

Francie swung around and headed back toward the school. "If you know all this stuff," said Arnie, "how come you want to get into pictures?"

She grimaced, as if she couldn't stand how dense people were about obvious things. "If it was my mother behind the wheel, he would have already asked her out to lunch. Do you get what I mean?"

"No," he said.

They parked about a block away from school. Francie opened her huge leopard-skin pouch purse and fished out a compact. She looked at her face in the mirror, wrinkled her nose in distaste. "As soon as I'm eighteen I'm getting it done. You should have seen my mother the last time they did her. They cut behind her ears, under her eyes, under her chin. They can take you in anywhere."

Out of politeness because she had given him the ride he said, "Your face is okay." He could see what was wrong with her face.

"You read music?" she asked.

"Not much."

"How not much?"

"Sometimes I look at the notes and they sound out."

"Look," she said, getting back to business, "we would make a team. You probably can't remember anything and I remember everything. So we work something out, and we go to Barry's party, A-okay?"

He got out of the car. "I'm not going."

He walked back to the school and waited on his rock for Arthur to arrive.

12

Kind Hearts and Coronets

BARRY LAY FACE UP on a bench drying out his pustulated skin. Mathilda had her foot up on the edge of the bench painting her toenails. He was trying not to look at Mathilda because he didn't understand the loss. He felt it, though. She nudged him with the heel of her hand. "Don't pout." She painted his thumbnail red.

"This is my mark. You belong to me. I didn't say I was abandoning you. Wait until the party. You'll see."

"I'm not going," he said.

Nobody seemed to hear him. Which was nothing new.

"Go psych out the new man," said Barry to Arthur. "Get a fix on him. In order to control, you have to understand the soul. My father says that."

Beulah was high-stepping on the bench beside Arthur. She moved with her usual slow grace, but when she came to the space between slats, she waved a hairy leg into the air, like a blind man's cane, trying to make a judgment. "Forget it," said Arthur. "Patterson was enough. Man, did you see him run?"

"He blew up," said Mathilda, painting a little toenail. "Like a tire with too much air in it. Like a tire that hits a hot streak of pavement and goes *splat.* Poor old Patterson went *splat."*

Red was writing answers backward on a Band-Aid stuck to his elbow. In red ink. That way he could seem to be casually checking the wound. Pulling away at the Band-Aid, he could see the answers and then re-cover the bogus scab. "What time is the party?"

"Go see who's taking over for Patterson," said Barry. "Dinner's at ten. We eat late, the way they do at Cannes. And after dinner, it's Arnie's night. A Persian delight, right Arnie?"

Mathilda kissed Arnie's cheek. "He'll see."

"I have the key to my father's best stuff," said Barry.

"Right on," said Arthur.

"But for now, go check out the new man. Watch him. See what frightens him. Look at his eyes. Always go for the eyes."

Arthur coaxed Beulah back into her jar and motioned for Arnie to come with him. When they were out of earshot, he said, "I think he's bananas, man. He's right off the wall. But his father has some good stuff. We're gonna have a smoke tonight."

"I'm not going," said Arnie. Into empty air.

The door to the English classroom was standing open. The new teacher was working at a cupboard, pulling down Patterson's little pamphlets and tossing them into a carton. It wasn't a man. It was a woman. Arnie laughed. That was a joke on Barry. She turned and smiled at them. She was younger than Patterson, although not all that young. She looked solid and self-assured.

"Oh, he ain't gonna like this," said Arthur.

When she saw that they were more than merely casually passing, she smiled and said, "Hi."

Arthur sauntered in. Arnie followed. Arthur looked with mild disinterest at the questions newly written on the board. Then he walked over to her desk and uncovered the jar and let Beulah out for a walk.

She put down her box of Patterson's little answer sheets and walked over to the desk. She bent over Beulah. She inspected. "What a splendid tarantula," she said.

Arnie smiled. That was a joke on Arthur.

"Fascinating thing," she said, watching Beulah walk the desk, "is the whole mystique built up around the tarantula. They used to believe that the bite of the tarantula was fatal. Unless you began to dance to a particular piece of music. Wild, frenetic dancing. You'd dance until you fell of exhaustion. When you awoke, you were miraculously cured. Only let's be scientific. The venom of a tarantula isn't all that poisonous. So you dance up a good sweat and you work it out of your system. They called the music the Tarantella." She wrote the word on the board. "Is he friendly to strangers?"

"She," said Arthur. He scooped Beulah up in her jar and covered her. "Watch yourself," he said, almost angrily, and he motioned for Arnie to leave.

Arnie started to say something, but Arthur said, "Shut up," so he did.

13

Wheeling and Dealing

"So is it a deal or what?" Francie followed Arnie in the nutrition line where he was waiting for his hamburger. "How about you and me go into Beverly Hills after school? I'll take you to the most expensive restaurant in town. Then you can watch me try on clothes at Monteverdi's. I drive them crazy in there. They can't stand me but my mother spends about a million dollars a year there and they pee in their pants until I finish trying on everything in the store. Then I buy this tiny small item. I used to rip them off but she kept telling them just to put it on her bill. So what was the point? Or if you want to hop a plane to Vegas. We could be there in an hour and come home after dinner. I did it twice."

"You're not old enough to gamble."

"I make up. I'm an actress. And I lose a lot, so they don't care. Is it a deal?"

Arnie paid for the hamburger and stuffed the change into his jeans pocket. "I'm not going to the party, so forget it."

"He's driving me crazy! I didn't *say* it was contingent! I just felt that you weren't having such a dandy time at home right now and my mother is on location with the bodies in the bathtub and the house is a morgue, okay?"

Over the smell of frying hamburger he remembered the heavy scent of Miriam. "Okay, but I'm not going to the party."

"I said I had a photographic mind! You don't have to repeat it *ad nauseam!*"

She bought herself some pizza and they both dragged across campus, beyond the football field. They are sitting cross-legged on the grass, looking out toward the sea. He thought of the wounded bird. He hoped it had gotten away. He didn't think it had. She laid herself full out, her arms over her eyes, and listened to him play.

When the bell rang for third period, they walked back without speaking.

14

She Thought She Was a Northern Star, Ever Fixed in the Firmament

THE BELL RANG FINALLY, and tardily they all shuffled in. They glanced at the new teacher without even curiosity. They fell reluctantly into chairs. They were in their post-Patterson depression, most of them. The tall boys had their legs carelessly in the aisles, watching the windows for sun or birds or action. Barry walked in leading the contingent, sorely disturbed by her presence, alarmed by the fact that she was a woman. Mathilda tossed her silken hair back a couple of times, like a temperamental racehorse. She glanced at the teacher scornfully. Arnie walked in after Red, his straw hair sticking out from under his hat, like a scarecrow.

They all sat, more or less, most of them in the wrong chairs. Just for the sake of confusion. She seemed to understand what was happening. Once she breathed in deeply, less than a sigh, more than a casual breath. Then she went to the board and wrote her name:

BARBARA BAKER

She sat on the edge of the desk, no indecision, as if used to what she was doing. Barry shoved his hat forward but watched her from under it.

"I'm sorry that Mr. Patterson took ill," she began. There were a few snickers. "But I'm here in his place, so let's get down to work."

Mathilda leaned forward to Red and pronounced, *"Dyke."* She heard it. They waited. But she let it pass.

Red raised his hand. He indicated the stacks of books at the front of each row. "Those are the wrong books."

"They are the right books," she said. "Please pass them back."

There was a little uncomfortable shuffle. "What book is that?" Red asked.

"It's a novel. Pass it back and I'll tell you about it."

"We don't read novels," said Red, as if he were ready to cry.

"Yes you do," she said. "Pass the books."

Red pushed his derby back on his head. "We do little questions in this class. They're in the cupboard. Do you want me to pass the questions?"

"I threw the questions out. I don't waste time on picayune nonsense." She wrote *picayune* on the board. "If nobody is gallant enough to pass books, I'll pass them myself."

Nobody moved. So she picked up a stack of books and began to pass them. She looked around the class as if she needed a connection and didn't know what it was. "Listen, I used to teach here. I'm not sure how I feel about being at a desk again."

Nobody said a thing.

"Once I read a wonderful poem about a man who left a picnic to climb a mountain where he could stand alone and throw thunderbolts, and when he got tired and lonely, he came back down and found that all the world was empty plates and overturned picnic tables. Do you understand what I mean? I want to come back to the picnic."

Arthur flicked his nails against the tarantula jar. "It's okay. We like the little questions. Just pass them out. No sweat."

"This is my class," she said firmly. "What I teach is my decision. That's what I'm trained for. Look, give me a chance and I promise you, I won't let you down."

Arthur opened the jar and let Beulah out.

"Back in the jar!" she ordered.

Arthur looked up sharply, confused and betrayed.

"Not that I don't love tarantulas," she said more softly. "But I can't allow pets roaming the room. It's too distracting."

There was a book on every desk. Now she sat on the edge of her desk again, swinging a leg, trying to get a fix on them. She held up one of the books. "I want to tell you a story. Once upon a time there were two men, a short, wiry, very bright man and a huge giant of a man who was very slow to understand things." A few of the quiet ones bent forward to listen. "This big man, he only liked to touch and hold furry things. Like a child. To stroke them and feel them. And the little man understood how much the world might hurt his friend and he protected him."

Mathilda gave her shoulders a stagy little shake. "We don't get *gay* stories in English. We get *gay* stories in Alternative Life Styles."

"Good," she said, leaning herself into it. "Is it possible for two men to have a deep relationship without being gay? What about the army? What about men on a work crew in Alaska?"

Barry woke up. Suddenly the explorer's hat was off his eyes, flicked away by a snap of his fingers. "What's going on here?"

"Something important, I hope," she said.

"Listen lady," said Arthur, "Mr. Patterson got very sick. You don't want to get sick. Just pass the questions."

"Thanks for your concern," she said. "But I have very low blood pressure. I want to tell you a story of two men in a hostile world." She wrote *hostile* on the board. One quiet girl in the back of the room opened her notebook and started to write. Barry snapped his fingers. She shut it.

"Give me a chance," she said. "I'll be here before school, lunch, after school to answer questions. If you honestly don't like the class, drop it. If you do, let's have some fun. I'm talking of two men in a hostile world who band together to find themselves a dream. I mean a big hulking giant of a man who needs to stroke furry things, who admires a woman's hair and strokes it and when she becomes frightened he accidentally kills her. I mean the story of a little man who loves his friend and knows that if they find him, they will murder him, not nicely. What more can you ask from a story? A poor confused giant of a man and his friend, two against an alien world." She wrote *alien* on the board. "Alien, stranger in a strange land. Anybody see the movie *Alien?*"

No hand rose.

"My father," said Barry, going almost nasal in his anger, "my father is Mars Fletcher!"

"How nice for you," she said. "Alien. Alienate. To push somebody close away."

He was almost speechless. He sputtered. "I said *Mars Fletcher!*"

"I know who Mars Fletcher is . . ." She checked her seating chart. ". . . Barry. His job is making films. And I gather he does it well. My father made ladies' blouses. Equally well. But the subject is not fathers. If we should decide to talk about Hamlet sometime, the subject will be fathers."

It was a small movement. Barry's finger. A little flick pointing to Red. Who rushed to the front of the room, carrying his book. He waved it under her nose, asking a question.

Half a dozen of them grabbed books and rushed forward.

The sudden rush caught her off guard. She retreated behind her desk, involuntarily. She shouldn't have done that. Red was in front of her, book open, asking questions. Mathilda flanked him, cutting off her view, saying that she had a dentist appointment. From over their heads flew paper clips, balled-up papers, an eraser hit the board.

She got her second wind. She pushed the human curtain aside. "Stop this! You don't pull this junk in my class!"

They all rushed to their seats. They folded hands on desks. Then suddenly all the chairs scraped.

"Honestly, not these old games."

They all dropped their notebooks.

"Come on!" she said. "Kindergarten tricks?"

Then she heard the small whistle. The class fell silent. It was a hint of a whistle, low, musical, a little crescendo of clear notes that traveled through the air. Every mouth was shut. Every pair of lips at rest.

"We have a whistler," she said, almost in admiration.

She watched that sound travel, moving her eyes, following it as if it were a trapped bird trying to find an open window. Then it stopped. It all stopped.

"You've made a serious mistake," said Barry. He stood up. He snapped his fingers. He danced into the aisle. He walked to the front of the room. He opened the door. "Out!" he ordered. They looked at one another. Then one by one they began to file out.

"This is ridiculous," she said. "You can't just leave!"

"We are," said Barry.

"But you can all be suspended!"

Barry flicked his fingers at the edge of his hat. He smiled. His face was a mass of painful red mounds but his eyes slitted with pleasure. "But how are you going to explain it?" He waved and said *ciao* and he walked out.

Arnie was just pushing out of his seat and straightening his hat when he heard the scuffle in the hall. Arthur came running back into the room. He slammed the wooden hall pass down on her desk. "I told you to watch yourself," he said angrily.

"But why?" she asked him, puzzled. "What did I do to offend?"

"No skin off my ass," he said. "I come on the bus. This ain't my school."

"Then you're here on a special pass. You can be sent back, you know that."

Arthur glowered at her, soaking her up. Then he said, "Him and me is friends."

"You and Barry? You did it for Barry? What is this Barry that you all follow him like lemmings?"

"Him and me is friends. That's how they talk at my school. My school is a good school. All my friends are there. Only they say, *Him and me is friends.* Not the grammar way. You get it?"

"I don't get it."

"Well I got it. My momma she gets it. She says, 'I killed myself in college for six years and your father killed himself for eight and we don't say that no more. Now I have one son and he says, *Him and me is friends.* And that son ain't goin' to no school where they talk crap.' Do you follow?"

She breathed in, pulling her nostrils together. "Yes, I follow. I do follow. So you *want* to get bounced. But why me?"

Arthur tapped Beulah's jar, he pursed his lips and made a kiss toward the jar. "Why anything?" he said.

15

A Diamond
as Big as the Ritz

"WHAT'S A LEMMING?" asked Arnie.

The headwaiter was having an attack of the hiccups. He snapped his fingers for a glass of wine. One of the waiters was rushing around the place putting "Reserved" signs on all the tables.

"Oh no you don't!" said Francie. She pulled Arnie into the middle of the dining room and chose a prime table. The waiter was frantically stacking the chairs against the table. "Oh no you don't, Alfredo!"

"Please Francie, no trouble," he said.

She spoke loud enough to be heard without amplification. "This is my friend Arnie Schlatter, Alfredo, whose new single is about to hit the air."

A few faces turned to see who they were.

Arnie took a chair. She was very funny. She fell into her chair with an exaggerated gesture of fatigue. "I am ex*haus*ted! They took that last shot about a thousand times."

Alfredo tried to shove menus in front of them. He leaned

over Francie's shoulder and whispered, "No wine. Absolutely no wine. Your mother said. . . ."

She started to laugh. "You pull that and I'll talk about the roaches in the ladies' *john,* Alfredo."

He was trying not to kill her. The headwaiter stood close by, his eyes on fire.

"Anyhow, I'm off alcohol. It's bad for the art. Mars said that if I come onto the set once more in *that* condition, I'm out of the picture."

The whole general audience turned in her direction, or bent to whisper. Arnie watched from behind the menu. Francie had her arm over the back of the chair in an air of divine boredom. It was funny. And it was a nice restaurant. He smoothed down his hair with the palm of his hand.

"We'll start with some good caviar," said Francie, "and Ritz crackers."

"*Ritz* crackers?" said an apoplectic Alfredo.

"And my friend Arnie, who happens to be the most talented musician in the world, would like some kidneys."

He choked on his laughter. "No I wouldn't."

"Well then, Alfredo will fix you something exceptional."

They ate scrambled eggs with truffles and mushrooms through fits of giggles. She told him how a Judas fish lures its prey into the waiting mouth of the sea anemone, and about pupfish, which lie dormant in dry lakes for a thousand years and then it rains and they come alive again.

"You know a lot of stuff," said Arnie, over blueberry crepes.

"I can learn a whole script practically immediately. You want lines? Name a movie, any movie. I'll give you the lines."

"I like the Judas fish better."

He was having fun. He took out his Hohner and got ready to play something, but he felt sorry for Alfredo and so he put it back in his pocket.

She left a fifteen-dollar tip. They sort of trailed out of the restaurant very bored and unconcerned. When they got out on Rodeo, she turned back bitterly. "When my mother goes in there, they fall over their feet and Alfredo kisses her hand." She looked at her own nail-bitten hand. "Don't you see why I have to go to the party? Once you get into Mars Fletcher's film, you have it made. I mean my mother would walk bare-footed a mile to get into his pictures. Only he doesn't do that much body-slashing in his films, if you know what I mean."

He was looking at a crystal egg in a window—pure solid glass but in the center was a small brass horse standing on its hind legs. He wondered how they got it in there. "I'm not going."

"You don't have to *do* anything! You can say you did it and then don't! I mean I'm not trying to seduce you or anything!"

"No."

"Just tell me why!"

Finally she gave up and took him home.

As he got out of the car he said, "You ought to wear your hair back."

At first she didn't hear him. Then she looked at him queerly, lifting her purple glasses and squinting into the light. She peered nearsightedly. "What?"

"Your hair. It would look nicer back."

He walked to the house. Once he turned and saw her still sitting there, sort of shocked, watching him.

16

Big and Little Women

FURIOUS! AMY SMACKED HIM on the arm. He loved Amy. He turned his shoulder toward her and made himself a willing punching bag. "Why did you *do* it? You know what Daddy said if you cut class again! You know!"

He leaned helpfully into the punches. "I forgot."

"And you didn't forget! You knew that Daddy would come home early from court to chew you out! So why didn't you come right home!"

"I didn't know," he said.

She stopped punching. Now she hugged his arm. Now she pulled him down on the sofa near her and held his hand. "Why don't you come to my room anymore the way you used to? We used to play checkers all the time. Why don't you want to play with me anymore?"

"You play chess now."

"Well I can still play checkers. We can play Monopoly if you like."

He tousled her hair. Her hair was silken and bright, like

Hal's. She and Hal had the same hair. Hal and his father had the same face. "I'm getting too old to play," he said.

"I love you so much." She stroked his arm. "Arnie, who's that girl? She's so gross."

He disengaged himself. "I have homework now."

She didn't try to stop him. "You don't *do* homework, Arnie. You never do homework."

It was true.

"You *knew* when you didn't come right home that Daddy would phone Montana."

"I didn't."

"Daytime rates. He was so angry. Arnie, why did you make him do it?" She patted his hair and stroked his arm. "Why can't we just keep it all the way it is. I don't mind. I'll always help you. Didn't I always help you? So why did you push Daddy?"

Arnie felt hot and uncomfortable. He was getting sick.

She put a hand affectionately to his cheek. "Daddy says that everybody has to fight his way in the world. Why does everybody have to fight?"

"He didn't mean fight *per se*." *Per se* was supposed to be funny. But Amy wasn't laughing. Anyhow he felt really sick. Maybe flu. He wanted to go to his room now.

"If he comes you'll have to say no."

"If who comes?"

"You *know* who. Just say no. Then Momma will argue and they'll have their fight and they'll put it off again."

"You," said Arnie. "You say it."

"I can't anymore. They won't let me."

It was really the flu. He was sweating and getting sick to his stomach.

"He'll be here for breakfast on Monday morning. I can't stand to think of all of them sitting around with Tante Miriam and everybody against you. So I phoned Tante Hannah in Mendocino. She's flying down now."

And his throat was getting rough. "Why does Tante Hannah have to be there?"

"You know why."

He could hardly swallow. "I don't know why!"

She reached up and stroked his hair. "Why don't you know, Arnie? Why don't you ever know?"

*

He was in bed with some warm milk which Arabelle buttered and sugared when the call came. His mother tapped on the door. Did he want to take the phone?

He took it in her little upstairs study. While he held the phone, she sat in her needlepoint chair twisting her handkerchief and watching him.

It was Francie. *"Listen, if you don't want to go to the party tonight, then how would you like to sleep over?"*

He didn't know what to answer. His mother watched him with glazed eyes, twisting the handkerchief, looking pained, getting ready for one of her discussions. She would ask him things he couldn't answer and then she would cry and say it was her fault and why could she help everybody else's kids in the world and not her own son. And she loved him. And what could she do to help him? And why didn't he come to her room anymore. And talk the way they used to. Did he remember that? He would ask a question and she would answer it. Why didn't he do that anymore?

He shielded the phone with his hand and spoke softly. "I'm not going to the party, okay?"

"I didn't say anything about the party. I just wanted to hear some music. You can have my mother's room, with all the mirrors. And I'll tell you more stories. I can't stand to be in the house alone."

"Isn't anybody there?"

"Only snoops and crooks and little spooky men who work in the garden. So do you want to or not?"

60

He put his mouth close to the phone. "I can't. We're having company in the house. My aunt is flying down . . ."

She had already slammed the receiver.

*

"Is it my fault?" asked his mother, for about the thousandth time. "Do I overprotect you?"

"I don't know." He wanted to phone Francie back. He didn't know her number.

"When you were small you always came to me. You played where I could watch you. If you were hurt you ran to me. Why don't you come to me now?"

He was really tired. "Can I go to my room please?"

"Why are you angry with me?"

"I'm not."

"You shut me out," she said. "You never let me in anymore. You hurt me."

He didn't want to do that but he didn't know how to stop. He waited until she was finished. She wasn't really finished, but she couldn't think of anything else to say, so he kissed her and he went to his room and locked himself in.

He thought of Francie alone in the house with the crooks and the spooks. He didn't know where to find her number. He didn't even know how to spell her name. He didn't know where she lived. She was probably not listed.

Then he heard the car door slam. Outside he saw the cab. He saw the driver open the door and Tante Hannah stepped out. Then he saw the driver take out her suitcase. She looked up to his window and waved.

He didn't know whether to laugh or cry.

17

This Alien Breed

TANTE HANNAH WAS a shrink. It always made him think
of headhunters. That was a joke on Tante Hannah. She was
his father's older sister and she was funny. Funny nice, not
ha-ha. She wore handwoven skirts that always looked fuzzy,
like the hair of an animal. Her blouses were batik from Africa
or other esoteric places, and she wore gri-gris around her neck.
Charms. Faces. Designs cut in yak horn. Yak. He had never
seen a yak. But he thought maybe a yak looked like Tante
Hannah. She had a great warm face, leathery skin and a handsome nose, gray-black hair caught up with a bone or some such
thing, like a savage.

She liked to sit in the chair next to his bed while he played
the Hohner, her fingers pressed together, listening and nod-
ding as if the music were words and she understood them.

She always asked the same question. "Arnie, how is your
spirit?"

He liked to play that game. Usually. This time he didn't
want to play.

"Your spirit is . . ."

He was supposed to put in a word.

". . . is . . ."

". . . a bird," he said.

"There are birds and birds. What kind of bird? Are you a bird in a cage?"

He thought about it. "No, a bird from the ocean."

"Ah," as if that was good. "Flying in from the sea?"

"A bird with a broken wing."

She thought about it. "And?"

"And it can't fly but its friend comes out of the sky and tries to help it back into the air."

"Can the friend do that?"

"No, because the wing is broken. The friend is really wild to get the other bird up, though."

"And . . ."

". . . and it pecks at the wounded bird."

"Pecks?"

"On the head. With its beak. Until it makes the bird's head bleed."

Hannah clasped her hands together, her eyes pained.

He nodded. Because Hannah always understood. "And finally it gives up and leaves the broken bird alone. All alone."

"And it feels how?"

Feels. "Alien," he said.

"Alien?"

"Alien*ated*."

"What does that mean?"

He shrugged. "Stuck in a place where it doesn't belong."

She leaned closer. "How did you feel when the friend from the sea struck at the bird and drew blood? Was it the right thing for that bird to do?"

He thought about it. "I guess it wanted the other bird to fly back to the sea. So I guess it was okay."

"If the bird bloodied its friend's head even worse, if it had to peck harder and harder and hurt its friend, but in the end if that other bird had the courage to fly back to sea, would you have accepted that?"

"But the bird couldn't. So it wasn't any use."

"But if it *could* have?"

"Then I guess."

"You guess what?"

"Yes," he said.

She left a space of soft quiet while the bird flew around in his head, those high circles, trying to make up its mind whether to leave or not. Then the birds faded.

"You know why the family is meeting this evening. Why Miriam came out of her doll's house wearing all her trinkets and baubles and risking the theft of her treasures at the hands of the lower classes. You know why Miriam is here."

He turned his face away.

"Oh yes you know. You know a great deal more than you let on, don't you Arnie?"

"I don't."

"What is Arnie? One quick word!"

They always played one quick word. "Nerd," he said.

"Another quick word."

"Idiot."

She did a little intake of breath, as if she had been sharply hit in the stomach. "As bad as that?"

He smiled. "Idiot savant."

Her bushy eyebrows raised. "Where did you hear that?"

"From a girl."

"Do you have a friend? Arnie, I'm so happy for you."

"It's not like that." He felt his face flushing.

"Why isn't it like *that?* You're sixteen. You're a man. You have sexual feelings like everyone else, so why shouldn't it be like *that?*"

His throat was dry. "She's just a girl. Anyhow she's weird. I just know her."

"I'm weird too," said Hannah. "So are you. By the world's definition. There are different threads and strains in families. I see the world differently from your father and my sister Miriam. I'm a Schlatter of a different color."

That made him laugh. "I know."

"But we are Schlatters. Very competitive. Very controlling. That's our nature. And you're one of our kind."

He shook his head *no*. It wasn't true.

"Oh yes you are. I saw what was happening to you when that bright little bird of a sister was born. All your mother's happy expectations. I saw you retreat into your little private cave. I asked your father to let me take you. Did you know that? I felt you belonged with me. But his ego is a terrible rock. And you're caught between that rock and a hard place. You know why they're meeting. They've been talking around the edges of it for months. They're sending you away. To train you. To raise your index in the American way. Numbers are the only things they understand. Numbers and letters and titles. They want to bring you into the mainstream. Your mother chose a music high school in Arizona. But your father wants you tough. You're being sent to a school in Montana. Do you want to be sent away?"

He put his hands across his eyes. "I don't care."

"Don't you?"

He didn't answer.

"I'm the bird who has flown in from the sea. Look at me, Arnie. I flew down from Mendocino to peck at your head. I may have to make your head bleed."

Now he opened his eyes. He leaned over to her and cuddled her and hugged her. "You couldn't."

"Oh yes I could. You're a bird with a broken wing and I want you to fly. You weren't ready before. Now you must."

"I'm not a bird," he said.

"Arnie you're not as slow as you make yourself out to be, are you. You have your music and your records and your fish.

And that sustains you. Like eating alone in your room. Because if you tell them what you are, they won't understand."

"They know what I am. I'm a nerd. Ask Hal."

She drew back and away from him. She looked at him sharply under those great brown eyes, under those bushy brows. "Let me tell you what you are. You're a tyrant."

Words betrayed him. Always. They turned on him. He shook his head. He didn't understand.

"Tyrant. Oh yes," said Hannah. "You're been tyrannizing this house as long as I can remember. And the time has come to make you understand that."

Words were traps. He shook them out of his head.

"Oh yes you understand. These family meetings, they're a farce. You have a verbal father with a tongue like a knife, and a verbal brother with a tongue like a hammer. And a fast little hummingbird of a sister. And your mother is so full of guilt she can't see the forest for the trees. Now you can't compete with that, can you, Arnie. You're sunk in a sea of words like that. But you are a Schlatter through and through. You don't just want to find a way to coexist with this family. You're very ambitious. You're bent on controlling this family."

The alarm signal was sounding in his head. "No I'm not!"

"Oh yes you are. And how to control them? Easily. Make them feel you're constantly being hurt by them. Keep them all constantly upset. They can't touch a fool or a nerd or a poor uncomprehending fool, can they? So you're free to strike out, in your own way. They can't hit you back. You make Hal uncomfortable every chance you get."

"It's not true!"

"It is. I've seen it."

He reached for his Hohner. He wanted her to leave. He wanted to play.

"Arnie, you've got more strength than you think you have. And you're smarter. So instead of fighting against whatever weakness might be holding you back, instead of building on your strengths, you intensify the problem. Arnie the fool. Arnie

66

the nerd. You feed off it. Only you've come to a wall now. No, it's a mountain. Silver Hills. The man from Silver Hills is coming to breakfast. They will send you away, Arnie. And you know it. You'll have to come to the table on Monday morning and you'll have to talk to him and you'll have to face your father and tell him you don't want to go. You have to give your voice, and you have no voice, have you Arnie."

He didn't want to listen any more. He began to play. He played out the afternoon with Francie. He played the empty house where Francie was sitting huddled up against the dark shadows that licked the corners of her empty room.

"Oh, you have music," said Hannah, "but they don't understand that voice. You must find yourself a voice to speak with."

He didn't like her this way. He wanted to get the old Hannah back. But he didn't know how.

He was still playing when she got up and left.

It was getting late. The sun was almost down.

He didn't seem to have any choices. He put on a pair of clean jeans and his Hawaiian shirt and he put his Hohner in his pocket and he put his hat on his head and he sat in front of the window waiting.

He knew she would come.

He saw the Maserati pull up and park. He waved to her. She didn't hit the horn or anything. The windows of the car were rolled up. She must have had the radio on. She was singing to the radio, making motions with her shoulders as if she were onstage with a mike in her hand. He knew that she would be singing like that until he came down.

He slipped down quietly. They were arguing in the study, talking all at once, going at it hard.

He walked out carrying his shoes.

Then she saw him. She opened the car door for him. The music blared out into the street.

He got in and pulled the door shut.

"I'm starved," she said. "Let's get something to eat."

18

Perchance to Dream

THEY DROVE THE MASERATI along the Pacific Coast Highway. The great overhanging cliffs had slid during the last rain. It had rained too hard and too long and the earth had soaked up too much of it and gotten drunk with it and the firm foundation of the earth was soggy. Porches of houses undermined by the slippage hung desperately waiting for something or somebody to secure them back up. Some pieces of houses lay on the hillside, having lost their hold entirely. Great boulders still lay on the road where the high barrier had been set up to hold back the movement of the mountain, bulging cracks where rocks had fallen and struck and bounced off.

The evening fog was beginning to roll in. Arnie couldn't hear the crash of surf over the muffled hum of the car, but his heart felt it. His heart smashed and pulled and churned like white water. It pressed his throat. He wanted to cry, but he didn't see how he could get away with it.

Francie shifted her glasses down to get a clear look at his

face. "What happened? Have a fight? I feel like that sometimes after a real toot with my mother. Listen, one time she
invites her boyfriend in, okay? I mean into my *bed*room. One
of these young guys who hang around her all the time. I think
they all have the same face. Like they were all done by the
same doctor or they're robots or something. So she's loaded
and she opens my door. I'm sleeping. And she turns on the
light and they're hanging over my bed and she says, 'Darling,
would you believe that I looked this way when I was her age?'
And they're all gawking at me like I'm some kind of corpse
they dug up. And my mother drags me out of bed and we stand
in front of the mirror and they compare what's going to happen to me when I get under the knife."

He only halfway heard her through the shell of his own fear.
"Is that true?"

She pursed her lips. She moved her mouth a lot over her
braces. She thought a lot with her mouth. "Most of it. Sometimes I dream things up and then later I can't remember which
is dreamed and which is real. So what happened?"

He thawed out enough to look at her. She was wearing silver
skintight pants, as usual the top button open, and a long-
sleeved sheer black blouse with silver sequins. Her sunglasses
were silvered mirrors, so that when you looked at her eyes you
saw yourself. He saw in her glasses, when she turned, his twin
images. "They're going to send me away," he said.

"Good luck. It should happen to me. But my mother hangs
on like glue. I think my grandfather left me a lot of money
and she's afraid to let go of it. Where are they sending you?"

"Montana."

She screwed up her mouth. "Montana? What for? Are you
into horses or something?"

"A military academy."

She turned her head. She had to move into the outside lane
because she almost hit an oncoming car. You could hear the
horn screaming as the car passed. "Are you serious?"

"It's a school where they raise your points. They say they can get me raised twenty points."

"Points of what?"

"To make me smarter."

"That's totally screwy!" said Francie. "I mean either you've got it or you don't! And I've got it, so what? I'd trade the whole damn thing for Mathilda's face and boobs! In a second!"

"My father wants me to know where I'm going. He wants me to fight for myself."

"I get the picture," said Francie. She drove with a kind of shocked look on her face. From time to time she turned to look at him. "Jesus. Military. That's like the slammer." She made a fast turn into The Mariner, which was a restaurant on the ocean side of the road.

"I'm not hungry."

"I am. We'll catch the last of the sunset."

The restaurant was semi-busy. There was a short line of people waiting to be seated. Francie took Arnie by the hand and pulled him to the front of the line. "I have a reservation," she said. "De la Paula. My mother eats here."

The waitress did a double-take. "We don't take reservations."

"How odd," said Francie, going slightly nasal and sarcastic. "Because I happen to have a reservation. For a window table."

The waitress thought about it and then she took two menus and led them to a table in a corner next to a window. Francie fiddled in her purse and took a ten and slid it into a napkin and shoved the napkin into the waitress's hand. "Listen, Montana might still work out okay. You go to Montana, then you wire me, I fly up and we split for someplace."

It was funny. It made him smile. "Where?"

"That's more like it," she said. "I was afraid for a couple of minutes that you'd died or something."

She ordered a mushroom omelet but only if the mushrooms were fresh and a stack of wheatcakes but only if there was real maple syrup. He ordered a glass of milk.

"So where would you like to go?" she said.

No single image presented itself.

The waitress brought a basket of rolls to the table. Francie buttered a couple of rolls. "I used to dream of a place. When I was thirteen. When my father was still alive."

"Is he dead?" asked Arnie.

"I hope so. They buried him. He was a stunt man. Boy, he had nerve. He used to set himself on fire and jump over a cliff into the ocean. Or climb the sides of huge buildings. He could jump a motorcycle over four parked cars. You should have seen him."

"Did he die in an accident?"

"If you want to call it an accident. He accidentally put the muzzle of a loaded gun in his mouth and pulled the trigger, okay?"

Arnie was shocked. He didn't know how to answer.

"I was thirteen. He walked out on us about a year before. On my mother, I mean. All that year I just sat in a corner and wouldn't talk. They thought I was autistic. Then I had this dream. I was sailing on his boat, he had this really nice boat, and we sailed to a jungle island. Like Tahiti or something. So I'm walking alone in this jungle and I see a savage. Really huge and terribly gorgeous and practically naked. Just a little loincloth to cover his thing. And I'm walking and he's following me, dodging behind trees to try to get a glimpse of me. Because he falls in love with me. Ha ha. So he follows me back to the hotel. And he sees my mother and all these other women, okay? But the point is he never *saw* a civilized person before and he doesn't know what's supposed to be beautiful so he falls for me. Then we sail home and I'm walking on deck and I hear these noises from under a tarp that's covering a lifeboat. And there he is. Hiding. Looking for me. Would you believe it? He stowed away just to be near me. Because he loved me so much." She put some jam on a buttered roll and put it on his bread plate. "Eat something."

The waitress brought the omelet and the wheatcakes. Francie

buttered and syruped the cakes and shoved them over to Arnie. "So do you dream or what?"

He cut at the stack with a fork. He wasn't hungry. "The sheep sometimes."

"What sheep?"

"I dream I take care of sheep. I have a dog."

"What kind of dog?"

"A dog without a tail."

"Australian sheep dog?"

"I don't know."

"Trust me, Australian sheep dog."

"I guess. His name is This Rock Egan."

She sat there with a mouth full of omelet. "You're kidding."

"I saw a science-fiction movie once, with my sister Amy. When I was little. It was this planet. And there were two spacemen. They were super-close friends. I think one of them was going to jail and his friend was trying to save him. So they get out of the space ship and they go to explore this spooky cave. And his friend says, 'We can hide here. But I want to see if it's safe first. Wait for me by this rock, Egan.' Egan was his friend's name. So Egan waited by the rock."

She chewed a little at the omelet, but not seriously. "So?"

Now he ate some hotcake. "That's all I remember."

"Did the guy come back for his friend?"

"I think he got killed by a monster. I don't remember."

"So you named this dog This Rock Egan?"

"In the dream."

"So what about the sheep?"

"I have this flock of sheep and the dog takes care of them. If one of them tries to run, the dog barks and rounds it up. It's a super-smart dog."

"And what are you doing all this time?"

He took out the Hohner and shined it on a napkin. "I play."

She thought about it. "Once I dreamed I had a gun. I kept it in my purse at school. When people were mean to me, I just accidentally let my purse fall open, okay? And they would get a look at the gun and I'd close the purse and I wouldn't say anything. They were very impressed."

"I hate guns," said Arnie. "Everybody in my house hates guns."

"You're kidding! Then why are they sending you to a military school? What do they think military is, for God's sake?"

He got suddenly frightened. His throat closed up. He put down his fork. "I don't know. I think they hate me."

He started to cry. He couldn't stifle it. He put the napkin up to his face until the feeling went away, as if he had to blow his nose or something, and then he was okay. He watched the surf for a while, and the birds running up and back following the fringes of the ocean, pecking for little bits of food.

Francie didn't say a thing. She put on her mirrored glasses and kept right on eating.

But somebody laughed at the next table. "Did you see that weird kid? He was crying. The kid was crying."

Arnie kept his eyes on the hotcakes. He poured on some more syrup.

Francie sat there frozen, with her fork in midair. Then she turned slowly and looked toward the voice. Arnie saw them out of the corner of his eye. Three sports types, very tall guys, jocks, with white tennis shorts and tennis shirts and jogging shoes and very hairy legs which stuck out into the aisles.

Francie looked around and snapped her fingers toward the waitress. The waitress got there fast. "Can I have a really large glass of tomato juice?"

She didn't start eating again. But she smiled. He could see his face in her glasses. He didn't know what she was thinking. When the juice came, she said, "Excuse me." She folded her napkin and put it on the table. She took the glass and she stood up. She walked over to the table where the jocks were eating and she said to one of the guys, "Would you happen to have the time, please?" As she bent over to look at his watch, she happened to tip the juice glass. "What the hell are you doing!" yelled the jock, trying to move his knees out of the way of the stream of red liquid. His pants were splashed red and juice ran down his hairy legs.

She moved with him, spilling as she did. "God I'm sorry. I happen to have this palsy, okay?" She put down the empty glass and showed him a trembling hand. "I mean I can't keep it still. You ought to contribute to charity for this kind of thing. It's really awful."

The jock was using very strong language for a restaurant as she walked back to the table. She fiddled in her enormous leather pouch purse and found a twenty-dollar bill which she left for the waitress. She nodded to Arnie to leave.

Everybody in the restaurant was watching them.

She made a beautiful exit.

They drove north up the Pacific Coast Highway, going no-place. At their left the wide choppy sea, all purple with little diamond lights. At their right the sloping cliffs. "My father," she said, "my father left about a million guns when he died. He was a stunt man. He was so beautiful." For a little while they didn't talk, just floated down that ribbon road that curved along the fringes of the world. "Now I go down in the basement and practice with his guns."

He didn't want her to hurt herself. He reached over and put a hand on her shoulder. She was solid, fleshy, and underneath the metallic material of the shirt she was warm. "You shouldn't fool around with guns. It's dangerous."

"I practice putting it in my mouth. Can you imagine the publicity? Daughter of the butcher-woman blows off her ugly head?"

"You're not ugly," he said.

She gave a snort of a laugh. "Says who?"

"We can go to Barry's party. If you still want."

She hit the brakes. They almost went through the windshield. She parked on the shoulder up against the cliffs.

"You can meet Mars Fletcher. Maybe he can get you into the movies. I think you could do it. I think you'd be good."

As she looked at him her mouth twisted into a half-grimace, half-smile, like the masks of comedy and tragedy in transition.

"I like your face," said Arnie. "I'm used to it."

She opened her purse and blew her nose into a Kleenex. She adjusted her glasses. She tried to toss her hair back with disdain, the way Mathilda did, but her mass of heavy wiry hair wouldn't toss. It bounced. Suddenly her face changed. The smile was the kind of open smile you see on a chubby jolly kid. The smile changed her whole face and body. "You sure?" she said.

"I am."

Already he could see the wheels in her head begin to turn. He liked to watch her think. She opened her purse. She took out a gold compact and surveyed her face in the mirror. She fiddled with her hair, pulling her stubby fingers through the tangles. She put on fresh lipstick. "Mars might want me to audition. I think this is a musical. A deeply symbolic musical. And I'm tight, really tight. I have to rehearse."

"Can you sing?" asked Arnie.

She shook out her hands, loosening up her fingers, as if she sang with her fingers, or was getting ready to play the piano. "I can't blow this chance. So I'll do a couple of numbers. We'll go to Gabe's place."

She didn't explain where that was. He didn't much care. He was happy to be following her directions. She started the motor. She made a U-turn on the Pacific Coast Highway that was as close to absolute death as he had ever been. They sped down the curving road to the blare of horns. She made a fast left into one of the canyon roads, a couple of hairpin turns on the dark road, and they were lost to the world, in an artery of a canyon that led into the rocks of the interior hills.

19

Little Gabriel Play on Your Harp

IT WAS LIKE TRAVELING in space. They turned and curved on the unlighted road. When the headlights hit the mountains, he could see layers of old formations that had been set down before the world hardened and tilted. He tried to watch the changing patterns of the rock.

"They're in stripes," said Arnie.

"What?"

"The rocks. In layers and stripes."

"Old sandstone, probably. The sea was in here once. Paleocene, Eocene, Oligocene, Miocene . . . *please* don't start me thinking of all that junk and getting my head mixed up. I have to think clearly." They turned onto a service road and drove into a small roadside settlement, mostly wood houses up on hilly roads and a sort of mini-village with a couple of lighted restaurants with names like Sunflower Place and The Sprouted Bean. She pulled into a drive. The sign was lighted but the windows were dark. The sign read Gabe's Place.

"It's closed," he said.

"My mother comes here with her friends. They're blues freaks. Sometimes Morris lets me rehearse before the place opens." She got out and walked up the path. She tried to look in at the windows but they were shuttered. So she banged on the door. Nobody answered. So she hit the door with her fist about ten times. Finally somebody inside called out "We're closed! Come back later!" So she kicked at the door for a while. Finally it opened a crack. The face that looked out was black, a prominent nose and a scraggly beard. "I might have knowed it was you. Go away, come back some other day." He tried to close the door but she already had her foot in. "You are a crazy woman, Francie," said the man who was trying to keep her out.

"I have an audition. I need to rehearse. *Please*, Morris, this is my big chance!"

He opened the door halfway. "You got an audition? You are one big liar."

"For real."

"Francie, you got a voice like a sick chicken. Who is goin' to audition you?"

She signaled for Arnie to follow. "I swear!"

Reluctantly he let her in. The little club was a cluster of round tables and a flat center stage. About five guys sat on the stage rehearsing. A few of the guys laughed and waved, somebody said something about time and looked at his watch.

"Francie," said Morris, "we are working on a little piece. So you just sit there like a quiet girl and don't make no chicken squawls. Or else come back later."

Francie pulled Arnie over to a table. "After a while he'll let me sing. Morris loves me."

None of them were young. All gray-haired. A trumpet, a fiddle, a clarinet, a piano, and Morris on the sax. Only it looked like a toy sax, a tiny instrument. He wondered if that was the one Morris played, or if it was a joke.

The piano led off. As if it wasn't sure where it was going. It made four or five starts, and finally settled down to one particular thread of melody. Then the drums shuffled in. And the clarinet. And the fiddle picked it up. They played around that melody for a while until they started to warm up. They played side by side, sometimes touching melody lines, sometimes running near each other, almost close enough to touch.

He understood all that. He put his fists down on the table and settled his chin over them and closed his eyes. This was the way he loved to listen. Alone. Private. He could see all the patterns. The way the little threads of melody moved and circled and joined and separated. Like a flock of birds, sometimes floating on thermals, sometimes leaving the flock and going separate ways, but always coming back together.

Then he heard the sound that came from Morris's sax. He opened his eyes. He couldn't believe that such a sweet sound came out of that small thing. The others fell back and the sax began its tale. It was as if Morris spoke to him, the message was so clear. His hand drifted to the Hohner. He took it out and polished it on his sleeve.

"Better not," whispered Francie. "He'll kill you."

It didn't matter what she said, because it was something he had to do. It was natural to do it. He licked at the Hohner, he put it to his mouth, he tasted it. He closed his eyes, he let himself join the flock of those birds, just floating after them for a while and then he began to play softly, catching somebody's melody, flying along side, unobtrusive and easy. Then he realized that they were leaving him a little space of his own. He needed that space. Keeping their melody, he played out Hal's face watching him from the crowd. Faces. Amy's face, always animated and alive until he came into the room, and then it became sad and worried. His mother's face, her alarm. The faces of her friends who turned and whispered. He played out guns and military. The blast of guns, himself huddled in a corner and the sounds assaulting him.

It belched up out of him, like lava, hot and passionate.

Then he realized that they had all stopped and were listening. Embarrassed, he stopped too.

Morris put aside his sax. He wiped his mouth with a handkerchief. Slowly he came down off the platform. He pulled out a chair from their table and sat himself heavily on it. He leaned back and wiped his forehead. "Where you learn to play a harp like that?" he asked Arnie.

Arnie looked at his Hohner. "It's a harmonica."

"Not the way you play it, sonny. That thing is a harp. We call it a harp. To play a harp like that, it takes two hundred years being hungry. Where you learn to play like that?"

"From records."

Morris rocked back on the two legs of his chair and gave a mock sigh. "He learned it from records. You hear?" he said to the band.

Arnie was embarrassed.

"You got Sonny Terry, Brownie McGee, stuff like that?"

The clarinetist said, "He's got a little Larry Adler and Toots Thieleman in there."

"Now that is fancy stuff," said Morris, smiling. "The old days, your poppa he gave you a harp and you would play out behind the barn, and you could play the hunter and his dog, you could hoot out the dog and bend those notes, or you could make the old train at the station cry. Then you got older, you found yourself a fiddle and a banjo and you was in business."

"Don't he sound like Gabe?" asked the drummer.

Morris wiped at his mouth pensively. "Gabe, he could play a harp like an angel. Only he didn't learn from no records."

"What do you think?" asked Francie. "I've got a few friends who might get him a recording contract. Maybe I'll manage him."

Morris gave Arnie a long appraisal with his rheumy eyes which had been too long in dark smoky rooms. "You leave this boy alone. Leave him be. Sonny," he said to Arnie, "what you want?"

Arnie wasn't sure whether he meant right now or in general. He didn't know what to answer.

Morris dragged himself up out of the chair. "Sonny, when you want to play, you come here. You come sit in with us."

"Thank you," said Arnie.

"You come and play for Gabe who ain't here to listen, you understand?"

He thought he understood so he said, "I do."

"Let me sing one now," begged Francie.

There were complaints from the stage. Somebody called that it was late. Morris was still watching Arnie. "Make it short," he said.

Francie jumped up on the stage. She shook her shoulders to get in the mood. Her belly shook with her. She ran her fingers through her hair. She snapped her fingers to the piano. "Cabaret," she said. Somebody laughed briefly. Only she was getting into it and she never heard. Arnie heard. She threw her head forward to shake out her hair. You could hardly see her face, there was so much hair. The piano began a little intro. She got ready like a relay racer waiting to pick up the baton. She waited for her place to start. And then she hit the first notes.

She was about an eighth of a tone off-key.

Morris turned away and put his handkerchief over his mouth.

She sang, "What good is sitting alone in your room? Come hear the music play . . ." She sang with total dedication and total exuberance, like Liza Minnelli. She shook her shoulders, like Liza. But her shoulders went one way and her womanly boobs went the other. She was doing legwork too. She put a leg up on an empty chair, the way Liza did it. Only Francie was too chubby. She looked out of joint. She was inviting you into the cabaret, to drink the wine, she raised an imaginary wineglass, her leg slipped off the chair, she had to pull it up again. She was working up to the climax of the song, where her friend Elsie is dead and when she dies she wants to be living in Chelsea and she wants to go like Elsie. It was a hold and a whammo high note. Morris's face was steady but his chest was heaving with laughter. Two of the musicians behind her were cracked up. She never saw it. She was enjoying herself.

She hit the last notes with her arms open wide to the world. Just enough off-key to make everybody behind her choke. They gave her some applause. She jumped down and shook back her hair and wiped her face and throat with a Kleenex. "So how was I?"

Morris tried to phrase a comment. "You got your own style for sure."

She grinned with satisfaction. "I told you. I'm an original."

She blew a kiss to the boys, she left a bill on the table under an ashtray. "Please buy everybody a beer."

They walked out into the velvet night. He didn't know what to say about her singing. He felt so bad about it that he put an arm around her shoulder as they walked to the car.

"You know where we could go after Montana?" she said. "South of France. I was in Avignon once. For the music festival, with my mother and these French guys. They have a lot of little cabarets in the South of France. And they have sheep. You could take care of the sheep during the day and at night you could play in these little cabarets. I could sing."

"Where would I get sheep?" he said.

"I'll buy them."

They got into the car and headed for Mars Fletcher's beach house.

20

All Things Bright
and Beautiful

THE BAY COULD HAVE BEEN Jamaica, not Malibu. Even
Trinidad. Hidden from the road by tropicals, backed by the
sheer rock cliff and fronted by a white sand beach with offshore rocks like sculptures that broke the waves into green
foam. The house had a wide veranda, with white wicker furni-
ture, and all the sea-facing walls were windows. A glass house
on a magic bay, where Mars Fletcher rubbed his fist into his
palm and dreamed his films.

Barry's little '65 Porsche was already in the drive, and
Red's tiny Renault and Arthur's Yamaha motorcycle. As
Francie pulled up the long drive, another car pulled in behind
them. They heard the crunch of gravel and the motor.

It was the white chauffeur-driven Caddy. But Mathilda was
not in it.

Francie did a double-take, she squinted into the rearview
mirror. She moaned, "Oh God." She parked and tried to tidy
herself up. She moaned "Oh God" a few more times. She
combed back her hair and checked the buttons of her blouse.

The Caddy parked, the chauffeur came around and opened the door. The woman who stepped out wore a neat blue suit, blue shoes, her blonde hair was gathered back in a smooth bun. She wore blue gloves and she held a little blue leather pouch under her arm.

Francie leaned out of the car window. "Hey, Mrs. Mattheissen! Listen! Mathilda slept over at my house last night!"

Mrs. Mattheissen ignored her and walked straight down the path and up the steps to the front door.

Francie scrambled out of the car. "She didn't phone you last night because she thought you were still in Houston! I mean, I just found out myself that you phoned!" She hurried up the path. "She and I were at a show when you called! I swear to God! And you know how religious my mother is!"

Mrs. Mattheissen rang the bell with her gloved finger. The chauffeur leaned against the fender, watching.

"Our housekeeper got the message mixed up. She's actually this Cuban woman. You think she understands because she keeps saying *Yes* without an accent. We were in by eight!"

Barry opened the door. He was wearing an ornate brocade jacket over his jeans. The jacket was a couple of sizes too large and it had a rather elaborate collar, like a gilt frame around a face that was badly humping and lumping into ugly mounds. His feet were bare.

Francie was making frantic signals behind Mrs. Mattheissen's back. "I *told* her that Mathilda was at my house last night! I mean, where else would she be! I'm her best friend and all!"

Mathilda came down the long corridor, drying her hair. She toweled the honey hair and she didn't see her mother—not until she was almost to the door. She must have just climbed out of the pool. A puddle formed where she stood, frozen, the towel still at her hair. Her suit was very brief—cut down between her breasts almost to her navel, and high up in arcs around her hips. Her mother said nothing. Just waited. Until she saw that Mathilda's vision was totally clear.

"I was at Francie's house," said Mathilda. "I didn't want to stay in the house alone."

Her mother entered the hallway. She circumvented Barry as if he were something odious, like a roach or a heap of garbage. She stopped in front of Mathilda. She slipped her blue purse under her left arm and carefully pulled off her right glove, one finger at a time. She put the glove in her purse and closed it. *Snap.* Then she put the purse back under her arm and with her gloveless right hand she slapped Mathilda across the face.

Mathilda didn't move. Nor made any gesture to indicate that she had been slapped.

"If you come home," said Mrs. Mattheissen, *"if* you come home, you come on your knees, hear? When I open the door, I want you on your knees. If you don't come home, then go to hell." She turned and walked back to the car. She got in, the chauffeur closed the door. Before he got into the front seat, he bent to get a look at Mathilda in the hallway. The white Caddy backed out, turned, and drove off.

Mathilda was still frozen, her wet hair snaked around her face, the hot hand mark getting redder.

Red checked to see that the way was clear before he joined Mathilda in the hallway. He looked like an albino in dark blue shorts. Arthur came behind him, a mahogany giant. Arthur was whistling between his teeth. Red said nothing. He was cleaning his fingernails with a knife.

Only Barry spoke. He smiled. He made a courtly bow and welcomed Arnie and Francie in. "Let the ceremonies begin," he said.

2 1

Games People Play

"WHY DIDN'T YOU TELL ME we were dressing for dinner, Mathilda! I mean it wouldn't have killed you to take three minutes to phone me, *would* it!" Francie, at the bottom of the stairway, lumpy and dumpy in silver pants with the top button open to accommodate her bulge and all those spangles, biting her bottom lip, consumed with envy as Mathilda descended the stairs. Mathilda, tawnily golden in a metallic sheath that was joined only at the shoulder and all that hair beehived on top of her head, with only two curls escaping, two little twists of wheaten hair over each ear. Slowly descending step by step with the kind of grace seen in deer that move through silent unpeopled forests. She rippled as she moved, fluid, a study in motion. Except for her eyes, which were blue and cold and hard as ice.

As she crossed in front of Francie she spoke to open air. "I *tried* to call you, Francesca, the way my *mother* tried to call you, Francesca, only you weren't there. You promised me you would be home to receive her call, but you weren't home, *were* you, Francesca." Mathilda linked her arm through Arnie's arm and pressed her warm lips to his cheek.

Francie bit at a nail that had nothing more to bite on. "I *was* home. I only went down to the basement for a couple of minutes."

Basement rang a warning bell. He wanted to say something to her about the basement. But he didn't know what to say. And Mathilda had him hard by the arm and when she felt him tug away, she dug in her nails to let him know where he belonged.

"Okay I'm *sorry!*" Francie whined. He didn't even understand her voice. He waited for the sharp crack, the whiplash of tongue, the rapier slash. Only it didn't come. Francie looked helplessly around the room until she found herself a bowl of nuts and she plopped herself on one of the big leather sofas. She said "Oh God" a couple of times and she lay back eating cashews.

"I'm not dressed either," said Arnie.

Mathilda hugged him. "You don't have to dress. It's your party. You don't have to do anything. You're so sweet, Arnie. You're never hurtful. You wouldn't promise someone that you'd be home and then cop out."

"I didn't! I just went down for two minutes! I didn't know the housekeeper had this Christian thing about lying, Mathilda!"

"Well, I know who my friends are now," said Mathilda.

Francie started to clown around, balancing the bowl of nuts on her forehead, being silly. "Oh *God!*" she said. "It was only five minutes!"

"I'll go home with Francie so she can dress," said Arnie.

Mathilda pulled him over to the sofa, shoved Francie's feet off, and sat down with Arnie beside her. She laid her head on Arnie's shoulder and picked up his hand and placed it against her cheek. He wasn't sure what he was supposed to do. "Tell her over there, the fat thing in the tacky pants, tell her I'll never forgive her in all my life for what she did."

Francie took the bowl off her forehead. "Then forget it.

Forget everything. Mars probably isn't coming anyhow. So I'm splitting."

The double doors of the dining room opened. "Oh, Mars is coming," Barry said. He was wearing the same brocade jacket but with a silk foulard tie over no shirt, black dress pants, and no shoes. "Mars will come and when he comes he will expect to see you."

Francie put the bowl on a table.

Arthur walked in wearing a white dinner jacket, a black high-necked shirt and a gold chain from which a razor hung, jeans, and boots. Beulah's jar had a red ribbon around it.

Red walked in wearing a black coat with tails, a pleated pink shirt, and dirty tennis shoes.

"When is Mars coming?" asked Francie suspiciously.

Barry came forward and offered Mathilda his arm. "Mars comes when he comes." He offered the other arm to Arnie.

Arthur offered a ceremonial arm to Red and they both entered.

Francie stood alone. Arnie tried to turn and say something to her, but Barry held him tight. Anyhow, he didn't know what he could say. He wanted to go home. He didn't know how to get out.

He was seated between Barry and Mathilda. Red and Arthur sat side by side around the circle table, leaving a lone empty place for Francie. Nobody brought Francie in. She stood in the doorway for a long while, looking with distaste at the empty chair, working her lips around her braces. Finally she walked over to the chair and fell into it gracelessly. Arnie waited for her to make some crack, to snap her fingers imperiously for the waitress, or to spill something on someone. He wanted to get her out of the room and into the dark night again. He couldn't stand to see the way she was caught, all her aura gone, the same wild hair standing out around her head, but no electricity.

The table was well set, with candles and an ice bucket with a bottle of champagne. Barry pulled the champagne out of the ice and dexterously popped the cork. The laughter and appreciation came mostly from Red and Arthur. Francie slumped, lumpish and glazed-eyed, watching the candles. Mathilda broke a piece from one of the rolls in the bread basket and threw it at Francie. "We're toasting Arnie."

"I didn't do it on purpose," said Francie. "You know that."

Mathilda didn't answer.

Arnie reached for a glass. Mathilda took it out of his hand. "We're toasting you. You just sit and listen."

"To Arnie," said Barry. He dipped a finger in the wine and flicked some over Arnie's head. "To the greatest whistler in the universe. And to the whistle of death."

"It was a joke," said Arnie.

"Life is a joke," said Barry.

"He's not dead. He's only in the hospital."

Barry drank down the glass and belched and filled his glass again. "This is Arnie's party. Whatever Arnie wants, Arnie gets. So bring on the oysters."

"I don't like oysters," said Arnie.

Arthur was clowning and rolling his eyes like a minstrel singer. "Bring in the oysters, man! Oysters is so *good!*"

"I don't eat oysters!" said Arnie in alarm. "Oysters make me gag!"

"Oysters make you horny," said Red. He mopped up some spilled champagne from his shirtfront.

Barry called out to the kitchen. "Mrs. *Dannnversss!*" He started to laugh. He had to stop himself. "Mrs. Danvers! Bring the oysters!"

Red started to giggle. "He calls her Mrs. *Dan*-vers."

"Mrs. Dan-vers!" called Barry.

"Who is Mrs. Danvers?" asked Arthur.

"Mrs. Dan-verrrrs!" called Red.

Francie reached for a roll and split it and was buttering it thickly. "She was the housekeeper in *Rebecca.*"

"She was the housekeeper who *loved* Rebecca," said

Mathilda archly. "She loved Rebecca so much she hated anybody who tried to take her place. She loved her even after death. Rebecca called her Danny." Mathilda held onto the edge of the table, as if for support, and bowed her head. A few coils of hair came loose. "She adored Rebecca. She must have taken care of Rebecca when Rebecca was a baby, held her on her lap, and brushed her hair. She was probably the only one Rebecca ever loved."

"My father," said Barry, "my *father* says that *Rebecca* is the total classic of the age."

"Mrs. Danvers," said Red, "was the spooky housekeeper who tries to push Olivia de Havilland out the window."

Francie was on her second roll. She had butter on her lips. "It was Joan Fontaine, not Olivia de Havilland. She tried to push Joan Fontaine out the window. Actually she didn't try to push her, she just tried to get her to jump."

"It was Olivia," said Mathilda. "You are full of crap, Francesca. You think you know everything and the only thing you know is crap."

"Joan and Olivia happen to be sisters, okay? They look alike. It was Joan Fontaine."

"You are so full of crap, Francesca, it is coming out of your ears."

"I was in the basement!" said Francie, almost crying. "I didn't hear what the housekeeper said. You know I wouldn't do that on purpose! I happen to be your best friend so why would I!"

"Well, you should have stayed out of the basement!" said Mathilda, her eyes also filling up. "You knew she might call! I have been doing things for you for a thousand years, Francesca! I have brought you here to meet Mars Fletcher, and what do you do! You get me in trouble with my mother! And that is really a friend, isn't it!"

Francie opened her mouth, twisted her lips around silver for a while, and then gave up and slumped back and ate bread.

The door from the kitchen pushed open.

"Ah!" said Barry. "Mrs. Danvers with the oysters."

The woman who carried in the tray of iced oysters wore street clothes. "My name is not Danvers," she said, not amused. "And I am not the cook. Cook is having a night off, as well you know." It wasn't until she set the tray on the table that she noticed the brocade jacket. "Where did you get that? Mr. Fletcher only wears that jacket on special occasions! That jacket is a precious antique!" Now she let her eyes drift around the table, trying to make out the nature of the gathering. Finally her eyes settled on the jar with the ribbon around it on the sideboard. She let out a little cry of alarm. "Is that a *spider!*"

"Please make the skin of the squab crisp," said Barry, "and don't overcook the asparagus, Mrs. *Dan*vers."

"Mr. Fletcher and I went over the week's menu yesterday. He never told me you were using the beach house. Why didn't he tell me?"

Barry was counting oysters. "I'm telling you today."

"I don't think Mr. Fletcher knows about this," she said huffily. "He'll be very upset if he knows that you're wearing his jacket."

Barry leaned back in his chair. The chair was rather high-backed and the collar itself was high, giving everything but Barry's face a regal look. The face was painful and swollen. He turned his face slowly toward the housekeeper and looked at her.

"You haven't been with us for quite some while," said the housekeeper carefully. "Perhaps you forgot to tell him. Why don't I phone him and let him know you're here with all your friends."

"*Who* will you phone, Mrs. Danvers?" asked Barry.

She was uncertain as to what he meant. "Call your father. Call Mr. Fletcher."

"*I* am Mr. Fletcher," said Barry quietly. "I have come to

live with my father now. I am *also* Mr. Fletcher."

She didn't know how to respond. She flushed. She considered. And then she turned and walked back into the kitchen.

"You said Mars was coming!" Francie accused. "That doesn't sound much to me as if he's coming!"

"It was definitely Olivia de Havilland," said Mathilda, putting an oyster on Arnie's plate. "Mrs. Danvers tried to push the mousy second wife out the window. I think she was a dyke or something and she loved Rebecca, whose name was embroidered on everything."

"Well, is he coming or not!" demanded Francie, with that hint of the old tonguiness.

Barry put several oysters on his plate. "Mars is coming, but it is not time for him to come yet." He slid an oyster off the shell and onto his tongue. He held it there for everyone to see and then he let it slide down. Arnie watched with a swelling of nausea. "Mars will come," said Barry, "when it's time. Mars never arrives until the scene is set. Now is the time for Arnie to eat his oysters."

"I don't want oysters," said Arnie.

Mathilda put two oysters on Arnie's plate.

Arthur poked at an oyster with his finger. "Oysters make you horny, man. That's the whole point. Eat the oysters, Arnie."

Francie was eating all the rolls. "Oysters are pure filth. They're the garbage cans of the ocean. Oysters just lie on the bottom of the ocean eating crud. If you like garbage."

Mathilda held an oyster up to Arnie's lips. "You are so full of crud, Francesca."

"I didn't say it," said Francie. "Jacques Cousteau said it."

"I went to the Cousteau museum," said Barry. "In Monaco, with my father, when we were in Cannes. Eat the oysters, Arnie."

Mathilda pushed an oyster between Arnie's lips. He kept his lips closed. She pushed the shell in and clicked it against his teeth. Red giggled. Mathilda reached down and rubbed the inside of Arnie's thigh. The shock of her hand radiated heat like fire. He felt his face flame, he released his teeth, the oyster went in, she bent over to kiss him, and the oyster slid down. "Good," she said, "we have to eat at least six."

"I'll puke," said Arnie.

"Then we'll have a Roman feast," said Barry. "We'll all gorge ourselves and then stuff fingers down our throats until we puke and we'll eat again."

"Man that is gross," said Arthur. "That is disgusting."

The housekeeper backed into the room, carrying the tray with the squab and asparagus. She was wearing a coat and a purse hung from her arm. She set the tray on the table.

"We're not ready for the squab!" said Barry angrily.

There were words hanging icily on her lips, but she didn't speak them. She turned and walked out. They heard the front door šlam.

Red called after her, "Mrs. Danvvverrrrs!"

"She's fired," said Barry. His pustular face was hot with anger. "She's canned. If I say so."

"Mars isn't coming," said Francie definitively. "I want to go home."

"Well you can't go home," said Mathilda, holding out another oyster to Arnie. "Because this is Arnie's party and you're Arnie's date. So just sit there and stop bitching, Francesca."

"You lied to me. You never expected Mars Fletcher."

"I didn't lie!" She leaned across the table screaming. "I never lied to you! Only you weren't there when my mother called! It was stupid, and selfish! Why did you do it!"

"I was thinking about my father!" Francie screamed back. "I went down to the basement for five cruddy minutes? How did I know she would phone that minute!"

"Now, now," soothed Barry. "No bitches. My father never allows bitches on the set." He broke off a little squab's leg and rubbed it across Mathilda's angry lips, teasing her. "It's all right, sweet. All you have to do is go home on your knees. We'll all go on our knees. I'll dress like that dumpy dwarf painter or something."

Mathilda drooped her head. "I wish I were dead." She dabbed at her eyes with a napkin. "I wish my mother were dead. I wish she would die and just leave me the house and the money."

Red speared a squab with his fork. "We'll get out a contract on your mother."

Mathilda's head snapped up. "Oh *can* you?"

"We'll get my mother to hack her up in the bathtub," said Francie. "Mad hackeress hacks up famous football-team owner."

"I mean can you really get a contract?" asked Mathilda.

Red pulled the squab apart to get at the dressing. "I was only kidding."

"Please! I can pay for it!"

"They never do mothers."

"I have a pair of diamond earrings my granny left me. Would they take earrings?"

Red poked at the dressing with one of his long nails. "I told you. They don't do mothers. Or sisters. All mothers are saints and all sisters are virgins."

"They *have* to! My granny left me those earrings in case things got bad. She knew my mother. She hated my mother. Her own daughter. She really had her number. She used to hold me on her lap and brush out my hair and say, 'You are such a sweet thing, Mathilda, and your mother is a tight-assed bitch.' She gave me those earrings just in case of something. Ask if they'll take earrings. Two carats. Pure blue-white."

"You shouldn't talk that way about your mother," said Red.

"Why the hell not, man!" said Arthur. "You ought to see my mother. She straightens her hair. She bleaches her skin. Everything she wears has a name to it. This is my *Anne Klein* skirt. Like that. Or the chairs. This is my *Eames* chair. Even the dishes. She serves dinner and she names off the dishes. She takes people around the house and names off the pictures and the pottery. Until she comes to me, man. Then she has a name for me. Shoo."

Red was eating the chestnut dressing out of the squab. "Barry's mother is a waitress in Tucson."

Barry's head snapped up. The conversation stopped. The little machine of his eyes lit up. He turned those eyes on Red.

Red put down the squab. "I was joking."

Barry reached for the carving knife. He picked it up, he leaned across the table. With a quick jab he buried the knife into the polished wood about a half-inch from Red's finger.

Red froze. He didn't move. He swallowed. You could see the movement of the Adam's apple. "I was only kidding."

Barry drew back regally and half-slitted his eyes. "Some jokes are funny and some are not so funny."

"Who decides what's funny, man?" asked Arthur.

Barry smiled. "I do. Mars and I. We decide."

Mathilda started to cry. "I want my granny."

Barry reached over and stroked her hair. "Then you shall have her, sweet. Phone granny. We'll send a car for her."

"I can't call her," said Mathilda. "She's dead. You know she's dead."

"Then if you want her so much, we'll call her back. We'll hold a séance and we'll have her back." He smiled one of his eye-slitting smiles. "That is, unless Arthur objects."

Arthur was sucking on a squab bone. "What do I care, man?"

"Niggers hate spooks. We all know that," said Barry.

Arthur sat there with the bone in his hand. He turned his eyes up to Barry. "What did you say, man?" His face was carved out of black stone. He put down the squab bone. He laid the flats of his hands on the table and began to stand up.

Red tugged at his jacket. "It's a joke, man! You know

Barry's jokes! Anyhow you're always calling yourself a blackass nigger! All the time!"

Arthur thought about it and sat down again.

"How come sometimes," said Red cannily, *"sometimes* you don't say *shoo* and *man?* Sometimes you forget and talk like your father."

"That's a lie, man," said Arthur.

"His father talks *Hahvad.* Sometimes he forgets and talks like him. I heard him."

Arthur went back to his squab. "My father is six inches shorter than me. My father is this little skinny guy who thinks he is so much, man. You know what that *Hahvad* graduate does, man? He operates on ladies. He cuts them up just like Francie's mother does."

"Not in the bathtub," giggled Red.

"He operates on these rich ladies. He takes out their females. And he makes a million bucks. And he's got the nerve to say I'm a throwback. Oh man. Ladies who don't need nothing taken out. And he does it for the bucks. And he looks up at me as if I'm the crud of the earth and he'd love to smack me only he's afraid. Man, I wish . . ."

"What?" asked Barry. Smiling. Pulling meat off a squab, stuffing it in his mouth. "What would you wish?"

"Why won't they give a contract on my mother?" asked Mathilda. "She's no saint! She fixes games! And she thinks God doesn't see her because God doesn't go to football games! I do, I believe God sees her. I keep a jar of her fingernail clippings in my room, just in case I can find somebody who will put a hex on her."

Barry wiped at his mouth with his napkin and folded it. "If Mathilda wants Granny, she shall have her. We'll call her back from the dead. We'll see if we have the power."

"The dead don't come back," said Francie. "Even Houdini couldn't come back."

"There are dead and dead," said Barry. "It depends on

whether we have the power. Mars has the power. Mars snaps his fingers and the whole world does what he wants. Because he has the nerve and the power. If we want to bring back Mathilda's granny, then we go for it. Mars says, 'Always go for it.' So we'll do it, then. We'll call back the dead."

"I don't like it," said Red. "It's not Catholic. I'm Catholic."

"Yes it is," said Barry. "Satan is in the Bible. Satan is a major character in the production. So we'll call on Satan to bring Mathilda's granny back to us."

"She's not down there," said Mathilda. "Granny is in heaven."

"Satan has the power over heaven," said Barry. "So we'll prepare."

"How do we call Satan?" said Red. "I don't want trouble with my priest. I'm already in enough."

"We find a snake," said Barry.

Everybody protested.

"All right, something else that crawls."

"How about a roach?" Red giggled.

"Roaches don't *crawl*," said Francie. "A roach propels itself on legs. They're *Blattidae*."

"Will you *stop* it!" said Mathilda.

"Go catch a lizard," said Barry.

"A lizard doesn't crawl either."

"We shall have a great lizard hunt," said Barry. "In order to hunt lizards you need to smoke. I have the key to my father's best Thai stick."

"A little smokie, man," said Arthur, "and we'll find lizards."

"We had lizards in the desert, when I was a kid," said Barry. "Mars and I . . ."

"Marshall," said Francie. "His name was Marshall Fletcher."

"That's a lie," said Barry. "His name was always Mars."

"I read it," said Francie. "Once I read something, I never forget it. I wish I could!"

"She reads too much," said Mathilda. "That's why her head is so fat!"

"I didn't *mean* anything! I never said that Mars wasn't great . . ."

"He's a god," said Barry. "Mars is a god. My name should have been Mars."

"Why wasn't it?" asked Red innocently.

Barry's eyes slitted.

Red threw up his hands. "I was joking! Let's get a lizard. Let's get Granny back and get on to the good stuff."

Barry's eyes were still focused on Red. "Sometimes you joke too much," he said.

22

Fire, Fire Burning Bright

THEY HAD BEEN CLAMBERING on the rocks for more than an hour. They had smoked up most of the good Thai stick. The coke was in the den with the other stuff. Mathilda carried a bottle of very old Cabernet Sauvignon and they carried their own glasses. Barry wore his explorer's hat and led the lizard safari. In the darkness the beams of their flashlights crossed and recrossed, like searchlights at an opening. Red, in his black tails, looked like a great beetle stomached on the rocks, probing for lizards.

Francie sat hot and sweaty on a rock, drinking wine. Arthur offered her a smoke. "I get asthma when I'm nervous," she said. "I don't want to start wheezing when Mars comes."

So Arthur went to pass the smoke to someone else.

"I want to go now," said Arnie. "I don't think he's coming."

Francie took a sip of wine and hiccupped. "Who?"

"Mars."

"He's coming. She was sore for a minute but she wouldn't lie to me."

"Why?" asked Arnie.

"Why what?"

"Why wouldn't she lie?"

"Who?"

"Mathilda. Mathilda might lie. She lies sometimes."

"There!" called Barry, turning his spot. All the flashlights converged.

"I'll catch 'em," said Arthur. "But I ain't gonna hurt 'em. They are pretty little things. I'll get me a lizard for Beulah to have as a pet. She can have her own pet lizard."

Francie's wineglass was empty. She looked around for more.

Arnie put an arm around her shoulder. "Let's go home now."

Mathilda hit them with a beam from her flashlight. "None of *that*. We're not ready for *that*. We'll tell you when we're ready for *that*."

Arnie turned away from the lights toward the sea. The moon was a fat crescent, and the sea in the grayish light looked the dull choppy color of lead. Around the Malibu bend the lights of another planet pinpointed, like colored stars. Mathilda came up behind him and put her arms around his chest. "Who else do I love but you," she said. "You never say hurtful things."

Red shouted from the rocks. He turned, leaned up against a boulder holding something. *"Aargh!"* They all turned lights on him. "I had one! I pulled off his tail!"

The others converged around him, turning lights on the lizard's tail.

"Look at that, man. I told you not to hurt it!"

"He didn't hurt it," said Francie. "The lizard just let go of it. It will grow back another one."

Barry climbed down and walked over to see the tail.

"Lots of animals let go of parts," said Francie. "Like starfish."

"Who's interested?" said Mathilda.

"I am," said Barry, inspecting the tail. "What things?"

"Sea cucumbers. If you chase them, they can let go of their intestines for you to eat instead of them. Then they grow new intestines back again."

"I'm sick," said Red. "Fish guts."

Mathilda perched on the rocks like a mermaid, in her silver sheath, her hair snaked down like seaweed on her shoulders. "Francie ought to let go of her head. Maybe she can grow back another one."

Arnie saw Francie's face. The dark look. The hurt. He remembered how he felt in the restaurant when he started to cry. How she called for the tomato juice. How she spilled it. How she took his hand and led him out. Now the hurt crossed her face deeply. He saw it in the moonlight. He moved over to where she stood and reached for her hand.

Mathilda caught their hands in the flashlight beam. "No, not until after Granny comes. You know the rules."

The hurt remained on Francie's face, but she moved to cover it. He saw what she did. He understood it. "You think I wouldn't grow myself another head if I could? In a minute."

Barry inspected the lizard's tail. "Can humans do that? Lose a part and grow it back?"

"They might. If you keep the scab from growing and prod it with electric shocks. They're trying it with frogs' legs."

Barry dropped the tail. He took a penknife out of his pocket. He opened the knife. "We'll try it on Red. We'll cut off a finger and put it in the light socket and see if we can grow another one."

Red turned and clambered higher up onto the rocks, like a black slug. Where his trousers hiked up, his legs were pasty white.

"Humor," said Barry, "is the highest form of art. Mars says that. But with Mars and me, what is funny to us may not be funny to someone else."

Arthur was laughing at Red climbing madly, searching for

lizards. "Come on down, man! That was a joke! Can't you take a joke! It's a white-ass nigger joke, man!"

"Got it!" Red called triumphantly. Mathilda handed up the jar. The lizard was secured.

They made a procession back to the house.

"Granny!" Mathilda held Arnie by the arm, leading him. "Granny come *back!"* He tried to see whether Francie was walking alone, if anybody walked with her, but Mathilda wouldn't free him to turn around.

23

The Headless Horseman

"IT'S TOO DARK. Turn on a light."

"The dead," said Barry in a dramatic lugubrious tone, "the dead abhor the light."

"What's *abhor,* man?"

"*Hate,* hate the light."

"Whatsamatter, didn't you see *Dracula*?"

"I saw it. Did you see where that guy ate bugs?"

"Cut it out, not in front of Beulah. That's all right, baby. You're all right."

"Silence," said Barry. "The dead hide their eyes from the bright sun, from the hot desert sun and the heat of the sand. The dead love dark damp places."

"Oh man," said Arthur. "Oh *man* will you look at her eyes! You can see the four now! Look!"

"They light up!"

The jar was passed around the table. Beulah's four eyes were glowing. Fingers touched. Hands. Somebody giggled. "Give her back! Who's got the jar?"

"We will be quiet," said Barry. "They have to know that we're waiting. *Silence* . . ."

In the heavy silence the lizard scraped the board where it was trapped under a glass cheese bell. It scuttled, scratched, tried frantically to escape.

"We summon the dead. Are all hands on the table?"

Arnie inched his hand over to where he thought Francie's hand might be but Mathilda leaned over to check what he was doing. *"Not yet,"* she whispered. *"We'll tell you when."*

"This is stupid," said Francie. "There's no evidence that the dead come back."

"She's trying to spoil it," said Mathilda. "First she spoils it with my mother and now she's trying to spoil it with Granny."

"Ma*thil*da, I just said . . ."

"I heard what you said! If you don't get into the mood, she won't come back! So why don't you stop messing things *up,* Francesca!"

"The dead return," said Barry, "if you have the power. Mars has the power. I have to have it too. So I summon Mathilda's Granny what's-her-name."

"Leticia. Her name was Leticia."

"Granny Leticia. Come, Granny . . . come to Mathilda."

The table rattled in the silence.

"Who did that?"

"I didn't do anything."

"It wasn't me."

"Well somebody did."

"Granny Leticia . . . come from your grave . . . no matter how deep . . . no matter how far . . . no matter if the flesh has fallen off the bones and hangs in strips . . ."

"Oh don't!" said Mathilda. "I don't want her that way! I want to see her the way she was!"

"My sweet," said Barry, "we are calling a dead granny. She comes as she is. This is a come-as-you-are séance."

"I don't want her in bones and skin off! Please! I just want her voice, to talk to her a little."

"Silence." The room felt heavy, the lizard scratched and scuttled. Arnie reached over and took Francie's hand. She grasped his hand as if she were drowning and hung on. The table jiggled. From somewhere you could hear a shuffle, the slush-slush of bedroom slippers.

"Granny?"

"Somebody moved the table. Francesca, if you did it . . ."

"Lay off me already, okay? I'm just hanging around until Mars comes and then I'm splitting. And if you don't want to see me again, that's fine with me."

The table fell silent.

"I didn't say *that*," Mathilda capitulated. "I didn't say I was wiping you out. You're my best friend. Only you did something bad and you have to be punished."

They strained to hear the sound. Was it footsteps?

"Ah," said Barry. "She comes."

"I just want to hear her voice," said Mathilda. But you could hear the steps. From where? Arnie held Francie's icy hand. They held on to each other while the steps shuffled, and the lizard scratched trying to make its escape.

"From the grave," said Barry. "In her shroud. With her skin in strips where it has come away from her bones. She will brush your hair with her skeleton fingers."

Mathilda screamed. "I felt it! It was her bony hand! No!"

". . . coming . . ."

". . . not that way! It's not Granny! Tell her to go back!"

"But it's too late," said Barry. "Once you call the spirits, the spirits come. I have the power."

"I don't want her that way! Anyhow it's not Granny! It's someone else! It's Francesca's father!"

Francie's fingers tightened. She was practically breaking his hand.

"Yes, it's Francesca's father, out of the grave, without any head, just the stump of a neck and his body!"

Francie released Arnie's hand. "I'm going home."

"Stay where you are!" Barry ordered. "If you leave now, I'll tell Mars you didn't have the nerve."

She didn't answer that. Arnie wanted her to answer, but she didn't.

"Nerve," insinuated Barry. "An actress must have it. And fire. Nerve and fire. She must be able to take the fire."

Francie didn't move.

"She has to be punished," Mathilda said. "She has to sit there and see the headless body of her father. All that blood spurting out."

"Is there blood in a corpse?" asked Red. "The blood is dry."

"It's embalming fluid," said Mathilda. "That's spurting."

"Not if the head's cut off," said Red. "You can't embalm a headless corpse. The stuff would all spill out one end. You'd have to sew the neck up first to embalm a headless corpse."

"No," said Mathilda. "The blood is still spurting. The way it was spurting when she found him."

"It wasn't. It wasn't spurting," said Francie.

"Oh yes it was," said Mathilda. "All over the room. All over her."

"Stop it," said Francie lamely.

"It wouldn't be a stump," said Red. "Not if he blew off his head. Only if he cut it off. And you can't cut your own head off. It would be shredded, with all the arteries sticking out."

"The blood was terrible," said Mathilda. "It was in all the papers. I mean how much blood there was. He was more than six feet tall. How much blood is in a six-foot man? Ask Francie. Francie knows everything. She's a whole encyclopedia of stuff like that."

Francie said, "Stop it."

"This is the magic circle," said Barry. "We are the magic. We have the power. That's how we killed Patterson."

"Patterson isn't dead," said Arnie.

"There is death and death," said Barry. "Now we must make the sacrifice to satisfy the spirits." The flame from Barry's lighter flicked on, illuminating the lizard. The little lizard scuttled around the circle of the glass dome, trying to climb, sliding, scratching. Barry lifted the dome and caught the lizard by the head. It was a beautiful scaly reptilian creature, iridescent in the light of the small flame. It twisted its tail, trying to escape. A small glass vial stood beside Barry's hand, a small apothecary jar of some kind. Barry uncorked it with his teeth.

"What's that? What do I smell?"

"What is he doing, man?"

Barry splashed the liquid on the lizard. "In the name of the power below. In his name." The lizard tried to twist away, but it was caught.

"That's lighter fluid! You're crazy, man!"

Barry reached for the lighter and suddenly the lizard was engulfed in fire. Chairs scraped away from the table. The lizard began to run, carrying its flame around the table.

"Oh *God,* man! What did you do?"

It was done. The lizard didn't run long. It sat burning, curling in the flame. The tablecloth caught fire.

"Oh God!"

"Oh Jesus Christ."

The light came on. Arthur ran with a pitcher of water and doused the fire. He bent with a sick face over the remains of the lizard. "Why did you have to do that? That was a living thing. That was a beautiful living thing that didn't do anybody any harm."

"Everything must be sacrificed to art," said Barry. "Things. People. Everything."

"That's a bunch of crap," said Arthur.

Red bent his amused face into Arthur's. "How come you're not saying, *man,* man? How come you said *didn't* instead of *don't?* I told you he was a fake. He's an artificial nigger. He talks *Hahvad* like his father."

Arthur walked over to the sideboard and picked up Beulah's jar. He checked to see that she was all right. "You shouldn't have killed it, man. You shouldn't have did that."

"But he should talk like his father," said Barry. "You can't separate a father and a son. Mars came out of the desert, like me. Away from the dry hot sand and the lizards. Every night I heard those lizards crawling up the window screens. Mars heard them too. Now Mars owns the world. Because Mars said he had the power and now he has it."

"Man, you're crazy."

"Believe what you will. I don't have to answer. Like Mars. Mars answers to nobody. Mars sits and listens and makes his plans. The way I listen." He turned in a circle and watched all of them. Francie leaned against the wall, a hand over her mouth, looking at the remains of the lizard. Arnie held her other hand. He was choking with the smoke and stink. He wanted to get out. He tugged at her but she was mesmerized by the dead lizard. Mathilda poured herself another glass of wine, her hair entirely down, her dress split at the seam. Red looked dwarfed in the black tailcoat, as if he had shrunk after he put it on.

"But this is Arnie's party," said Barry. "The séance is over. Arnie is the silent spirit. He never speaks. He wants and he doesn't speak. But whatever Arnie wants, Arnie gets. What does Arnie want?"

He didn't answer.

"Perhaps Arnie is a lizard on a rock. He just sits and listens and then scampers away."

"I'm not," said Arnie.

"He speaks!" said Barry. "He listens and he speaks and he whistles. But does he feel?"

"He does feel," said Mathilda. "He loves me."

"He worships the unattainable goddess, is that right, Arnie?"

He couldn't answer.

"Come," said Barry, "we must know what you think. Arnie must think and hope and dream something. He must dream like the rest of us. All things start in dreams. That's what Mars says. Mars keeps a dream book. What does Arnie dream?"

Francie squeezed his hand to warn him. He didn't know for what.

"Arnie dreams . . . does he dream of Mathilda? Does he dream of Mathilda walking into his room?"

"Hot dreams?" snickered Red. "Wild dreams."

They all waited. Arnie felt like the lizard under the glass cover. "Arnie dreams . . ." Barry prompted.

". . . of the planet," Arnie said. Francie dropped his hand and turned away.

"*What* planet," asked Barry, with interest.

He shouldn't have said it. He always said things he shouldn't have said, but he wasn't sure why he shouldn't have said them. He looked to Francie for an answer, but she was turned away.

"Where is this planet? What kind of planet?"

"Planet of the apes," said Red.

"Shut up," said Barry. "This is Arnie's party and we're Arnie's friends. And he has to trust his friends, right?"

"Right," said Red.

"We are a magic circle. If he lies, he breaks the circle, and the party is spoiled. Right?"

"The magic is us," said Mathilda, resting her head on his shoulder. "He can tell me. Am I still your friend, Arnie?"

He didn't answer. He wasn't sure.

"Did I ever hurt you? Ever?"

She did once. But he could have been wrong. He wasn't sure.

"You have to tell," she said. "It's part of the game."

Everyone waited.

"Where is the planet?" said Barry.

"Just a place I dream about," Arnie said.

"And what is the planet like?" said Barry. "The planet is like . . ."

"Everybody on it looks like me."

Francie had her head averted.

Red giggled.

"Everybody?" said Barry. "Even the women?"

"No," said Mathilda. "The women look like Francesca."

Red was doubled over with laughter. "The planet of the nerds," he choked. "The planet of the dogs. Doggy-Nerdy Land."

"Cut it out, man," said Arthur.

Mathilda smiled and put a finger to her lips. "That's not nice."

Red couldn't leave it. "Doggy-Nerdy Land! Attack of the Nerds!"

"Why don't you shove it," said Francie. "I'm going home."

"You don't have to go now," said Mathilda. "The punishment is over. The sacrifice has been made. I forgive you."

"You know what you can do," said Francie.

"It's all over. Now Mars can come. Now you've passed the test. Now you can audition and get your part and buy your own place and your own car and you can tell your mother to shove it. That's what you want, Francesca."

Francie looked beaten. She closed her eyes. She leaned against the wall with eyes closed. Yes. That's what she wanted.

"The desert is such a quiet place at night," said Barry. "Quiet as death. You can hear the voices of the dead in the desert. The old Indians who were buried there. And the lizards. Everywhere. It's so hot in the desert. Only hot dead silence and lizards."

Francie was defeated. "The whole world is a grave," she said emptily. "If you think of all the people who died since the beginning of time. People who got old. People in wars. People who killed themselves. You can figure that every place you walk is a grave with dead bodies under it."

"I forgive you now," said Mathilda. She walked unsteadily over to Francie. She put arms around Francie's shoulders and embraced her. Francie stood there for a while, just letting her. Then reluctantly she raised her own arms and embraced Mathilda. They stood there like two slow dancers holding each other.

"My father is coming," said Barry. "Mars trusts me. He only

has to look at my face and he understands. Because I am flesh of his flesh and so we don't need to speak to each other. That's why he's going to let me work on his next picture."

"Will he be here soon?" asked Francie.

"We'll hold the audition now," said Barry. "You'll audition for Mars. And for Arnie."

"I don't feel good," said Arnie. "I'd like to go home."

Nobody heard him.

"You'll have a smoke," said Barry. "You killed Patterson and you'll have your reward. You'll have a smoke of the good stuff and you'll find your planet. So we'll go into the other room now and Francie will begin her audition."

"I'll audition when Mars comes."

"But that's not the plan. When Mars comes the stage must be set. The scene must always be set for Mars. So Arthur goes and mixes the stuff, and Mathilda gets the booze and clean glasses, and Red sorts out the pills so we don't get rainbows mixed with 'ludes, never mix, never worry, and Francie hunts for the right tape so that we can have music."

"Does Mars want me to sing?"

"She'll sing 'Cabaret,'" said Mathilda. "That's her best number."

"And she'll dance," said Barry, "and she'll act."

"Will I sing first?"

"No," said Barry. "First you'll strip."

24

Invitation to the Dance

BEULAH SAT IN HER JAR on the bar, several of her legs up against the glass on Arthur's side while Arthur opened little tin containers of powdered parsley and mixed them in a glass bowl with the white stuff. On the mirror, he had the coke and the razor to chop it with. "Man, I always wanted to tend bar."

Barry reclined on a long lounge chair, smoking the last of the Thai stuff. "My father," said Barry, taking a deep drag and then handing the cigarette over to Mathilda, who sat on the floor with her back against his chair, "my father says that every artist must stand naked on the table. He tells that to every new actress. Stand naked on the table."

Mathilda handed the cigarette to Arnie.

"I don't smoke."

She leaned over and put the cigarette to his lips. "Just take the littlest puff for Mathilda, sweet."

He took a minimal puff and blew it out. He was worrying about Francie, who stood in the center of the room, dancing with herself, hugging herself, looking miserable. "He didn't mean naked *literally,*" said Francie. "That's just a way of say-ing things, like he wants an actress to be naked in the way she acts." She was moving slowly through space. "Naked feelings." She was stalling for time.

"But I want you to dance," said Barry. "I want to see the configurations of your body. The way an artist sees a body. A director like Mars Fletcher is an artist with bodies. He molds bodies."

"I *know* that," said Francie.

"Then strip," he said.

Arnie tried to get up. He wanted to leave the room, just to go to the can. But Mathilda held him back. She had a bowl of olives on the floor, big black oily Greek olives. She was trying to feed him olives. "Olives make you sensuous."

Arthur carried the mirror over to where they sat. Red was already stoned out on bourbon. Barry reached into his wallet and took out a fresh fifty-dollar bill. He smoothed it out and then rolled it into a round straw. "Who first?"

"Me," said Red.

He leaned over the mirror and snorted through the fifty-dollar straw. He started to choke, and then he lay back smiling. "Oh man."

"What if something holds him up and he doesn't get here," said Francie.

"I said he would," said Mathilda. "I'm your friend again. So either you trust me or you don't."

"I trust you," said Francie, begrudgingly, making her slow circles, holding herself tight to hide what was beneath her clothes, moving around the room in those slow, lazy circles.

The room was airless. It was getting closer. Arthur leaned over and took a good snort. He laughed and sat on the floor with Beulah's jar between his legs. Mathilda shoved an olive in Arnie's mouth. He chewed on the oily thing.

Mathilda got up and put a tape on the machine. It was Liza Minnelli doing the lead song from *Cabaret*. Francie was still moving in slow circles, trying to decide. As she passed, Arnie tried to catch her eye, or give her a signal, but she went blindly around and away. The music began to fill the room. Mathilda leaned over and took a sniff through the tube and threw back her hair and settled back, holding Arnie's hand with one hand and Barry's with the other. "Now," she said.

"Time," said Barry. "You have a whole career starting now. If you have the nerve."

She had been turning for a while. She was hot, her skin oily and sweated. She began to dance, clumsily, heavily, slowly, she stood first on one foot and then the other. Not the way she danced at Gabe's Place, with all the verve and enthusiasm. Arnie wasn't even sure this was Francie. This was some shell of Francie, some leftover thing. Mathilda was watching, her eyes cold hard glass. Red's eyes were closed. He tapped a hand to the music.

As she turned, Francie reached up and unbuttoned one button of her blouse, exposing the heavy cleavage of her breasts, her full shoulders. He was ashamed. He wanted her to stop. He wanted to get up and take her hand and get her away from there to the South of France where the dog and the sheep were waiting. Or he wanted to take her to the planet cave, and he'd go inside to make sure it was safe for her. But Mathilda held him down. Mathilda and the weight of the air . . . something.

She unbuttoned the second button. The blouse fell open. Framed in the sequined blouse, those heavy matronly breasts and the little fat tire around her middle. Red leaned over and fell to the floor laughing. But she didn't seem to hear it. She had already withdrawn herself into a world where Mars Fletcher watched her and tested to see if she had the stuff.

"Don't," Arnie said.

Barry lifted his head and heard Arnie; listened to see what else he'd say. He winked at Mathilda and Mathilda smiled.

"Don't," Arnie said again. Francie swayed, her breasts swaying to all the mocking eyes. He couldn't bear it. He stood up.

He just walked over to where she was doing her silent dance and took her hand. "This is my party. I want to go outside now."

Arthur wagged a finger. "Horny horny Arnie."

"Not *yet!*" said Barry. "We'll tell you when!"

But he pulled her across the room.

Francie was still dancing, eyes shut, moving with Arnie across the room as if they were dancing together. The rest of them were cracked up, convulsed with laughter. Red was choking with the hiccups. Arnie didn't understand the joke. He never did. He thought things were funny and other people didn't. Or he was serious, like now, and they laughed. Always. He pulled her to the patio door.

Francie came up slowly out of her fog. She was suddenly aware of being pulled by him, and of her nakedness. Her free hand fluttered toward her breasts. "What are you doing?"

He pulled her between the drapes to the patio outside and closed the door behind them.

"Leave me alone!" she shouted. "I'm auditioning!"

"No, you're not. They're making fun of you."

She yanked her hand away. "Why are you messing in? Who asked you to mess in! You don't understand how they do things in the industry! This is the way things happen!"

"It's not." He tried to catch hold of her hand again but she backed away from him.

"Who told you to mess things up! Now Mars won't want me!" She tried to slap him but he ducked. She began to run away from him but he followed her and caught her arm.

The drapes from the house were open now. They were all standing at the window, laughing. Framed in the window, like his mother and Tante Miriam and Hal, that first day. All at the window. All the faces staring at him.

Nerd! Nerd! Nerd!

25

On the Beach

ARNIE DRAGGED FRANCIE half-stumbling, half-falling, across the sand. One of her shoes came off. He left it. He pulled her away from the house. "Leave me alone!" she screamed. Her blouse hung from one shoulder. He tried to put an arm around her for support but she pushed him away. "What are you doing! I'm auditioning for Mars! It's a chance of a lifetime! Why did you stop me!"

He tried to maneuver the blouse back on her arm. "You weren't," he said.

"You don't under*stand!*" she said. "You don't know what my mother has to do to get her hacking jobs! This is the way they do it!"

He managed to get the blouse over her shoulders. "No it isn't."

Finally she stopped struggling. She fell onto her knees in the still-warm sand. The waves made a couple of spills onto the beach. She looked toward the sea. "They were auditioning me," she said emptily.

"They were making fun." Slowly he buttoned the blouse. She didn't try to stop him. She sat on her knees, her head hung forward. He got down on his knees also, closing the blouse, smoothing it.

"What do *you* know," she said. "You don't know about the movie business."

"I know about that." She was crying now. Strands of her hair stuck to her face. He smoothed back her hair from the sides of her face. He needed something to tie it back. He took off his shoe and pulled out a lace. He came behind her and twisted her hair into a round curl and then he tied it with the lace. He wanted to wash her face. It was sticky with tears and mascara. He didn't have a handkerchief. He pulled out his shirt and he ran down to the edge of the surf and he bent and dipped the shirttail in the water. She was still on her knees when he returned, not moving much. He washed her face the way you wash a child's face, softly, without abrasion, a little piece at a time. She seemed very tired. She swayed a little, looking out to the quiet sea.

"Flounders, for instance," she said. "I mean you try to sleep at night and suddenly these flounders come into your head. Did you ever see a flounder?"

She sat down on the sand and he sat beside her. Easily, he put an arm around her and pulled her to safety against him. "I once ate a flounder. When we were in New York. It's good."

"See, it's this flat fish. And it lives on the bottom of the sea. It lies flat and it hides and nobody hurts it because they can't see it lying there on the bottom. But when it's born it's just like a regular fish with eyes on both sides of its head. Then it drops to the bottom and turns itself over flat. So this one dumb eye is on the bottom. Then one day this bottom eye begins to move. It moves around the flounder's head until both eyes are on the top. Two crazy eyes on the top of one head and now this fish can just lay on the bottom of the ocean and hide."

"Is that true?" said Arnie.

"... and lobsters. Did you know lobsters did it face to face like humans? I mean, try to picture it. All clicky and snappy with their little hard lobster things. I mean try to get a good night's sleep and the minute you drop off you can almost hear all this clicking ..." She stopped. She raised her face to the moon. "He never meant for Mars to come. I was just the floor show, right? So what do I care. I've been screwed by worse rats than Barry. You want me to tell you all the other things that happened to me? I mean, this is nothing."

"I want to hear about fish," he said.

"Why can't people be like flounders," she said. "Why can't their faces shift and change so that they can be camouflaged in the world, so they'll look like all the other fish and they won't be hurt so much."

He stroked her face and her hair and her shoulder.

She leaned against him. "We're some pair all right. The fantastic duo. An idiot savant and a mental basket case."

He kept smoothing her hair with the flat of his hand. "A lot of people are weird. My Tante Hannah is weird and she's a shrink. Like me. I'm a Schlatter of a different color. She said I was." He hoped that was a joke. It sounded like a joke to him. She didn't laugh though.

"You want a real joke?" she said. "A ha-ha joke? Something that will really crack you up?"

"I want to hear about the fish. I like all that stuff."

"My mother, she thinks I'm some kind of nympho. I've been telling her horror stories since I was fifteen. So she put me on the Pill. She even had a diaphragm fitted. I mean she figures she'd better get me set before I bring some little monster home, get it? Only I'm still a virgin. Does that give you a laugh or not?" She lay back on the sand and spread out her arms. "I'm the biggest joke in town. And if you tell Mathilda I'll kill you."

"I won't tell her."

The moonlight gave a grayish, unreal cast to her face. "I'm a freak. Practically everyone in town is afraid to walk on the street because they might get raped. I'm available, I mean available, and nobody wants it. Does that get at you?" Her voice was brittle but her eyes were hurt. She looked to Arnie for the answer.

"How can lobsters do it face to face?" asked Arnie. "A lobster can hardly bend." He stretched out on the sand beside her, the soft and silent sand, only the little splashing of the low-tide surf. And around the Malibu bend the lights of the other world.

She let him stroke her face and her hair. She didn't mind. "Don't you ever dream of blowing something up? I mean, don't you ever dream that your folks will die and leave you the money? Or that you have your face changed and the doctors and all the nurses are standing around the operating table unwinding the bandages and then the last bandage comes off and the nurses all gasp at your total unbelievable beauty, because you're so gorgeous. Don't you wish things like that?"

"Sometimes I wish I were Hal," he said.

She lifted her head. "You're kidding! That blob?"

He stroked her arm. "I'm really glad you're back again. For a while in there I thought that you were dead or something."

She laughed. It was a joke and she got it.

She turned toward him. "That planet. I wish we were on it. Nerdy-Doggy land."

"Wait for me by this rock, Egan." He was playing on her soft arm, like a piano, trying to hear the notes he was playing. He put his face closer to hers. She smelled yeasty, underarm, unshaved, but nice, like the ground on a hot day, like animals he loved, or babies. Then he took out his Hohner and began to play. You could see birds crossing the crescent moon, so he played the bird that was lost. He wondered did birds stay together all their lives? He played that. He played the soft tide. He played that he once remembered a very big lake, maybe when he was a little kid. At the fringes of this big lake, floating on the marges of the foamy tide, was a cottage cheese carton. It was a closed carton so it bobbed and dipped like a little boat. He watched it following the movement of the lake

tide, moving in and out with the splashes, dipping and bob-
bing but never turning over. He remembered watching it for
the longest time, waiting to see if it would tip, and finally with
one big splash it got beached. He was so happy that it finally
got to rest, and then another wave came and lifted it back to
its fringy foamy journey. He played that for a while. Then he
began to play deeper things. He turned and saw her lying on
the sand under the moon, the tightness of her blouse, how it
framed her breasts, and they sang a song to him as deep as
his music. Then he stuffed his Hohner in his pocket and put
his face down to her breasts and rested there.

She let him. She even put up a hand and touched his hair.
Then he lifted his head and she put her arms around his neck.
He wanted to kiss her but there was too much silver in her
mouth. So he kissed the soft chubby side of her neck. He kissed
that for a long sweet time. He waited for somebody to say stop,
or for some blow to fall, or a sharp voice, or laughter, or
something. Nobody said stop. He was on that other planet with
her. Around them only the hushed voices of the others, all the
other tall lanky straw-haired men and all the other soft wild-
haired bright-minded women. He reached over and unbuttoned
the buttons that he had recently closed. She just lay back and
waited. He wanted to say something important to her but he
didn't know the thing to say. Anyhow he was afraid that if
he spoke it would vanish. For a while he looked at her breasts
in the moonlight. He wanted to touch them but he was afraid
she would tell him not to. He wanted to be in the sanctuary
of his own room with the door locked and her beside him and
the familiar blanket covering them both, and holding her and
touching her, making her laugh, taking away the memories
of headless bodies . . . he wanted . . .

"I tried a thousand times to kill myself," she said. "I ended
up in the hospital twice."

He put his hand on her warm skin, along the perimeter of
the hill of her breast.

"I'm afraid of guns. They remind me of my father. I tried

putting the gun in my mouth but I got too scared, so I took her pills. She takes about a dozen kinds of pills. But they went and pumped me out. I guess I never take enough. It's just that I swallow the first batch and then one of these crazy ideas comes into my head. Like maybe I'm just some kind of worm and I'll roll myself up in a cocoon and when I hatch I'll come out different. I want to be different. I don't want people to look at me that way anymore. You know?"

"Yes," he said. He wasn't much hearing the words. He let his fingers move higher and higher, and he came closer to her. He kissed her mouth near her cheek. She put both arms around him and held on as if she were drowning.

This was the different planet.

He didn't know the right moves, but a primitive knowledge moved him.

They settled into the rhythm of the sea. He heard her say "Oh," once, as if there were something he was explaining that she didn't quite understand and suddenly she understood it.

He didn't know when the laughter started.

She must have heard it first. She pulled up her head and listened, she half-sat, leaning back on her elbows.

Then he heard it.

Muffled laughter. It stopped, then they heard it again.

She pulled herself away. "Oh Jesus," she moaned.

He was confused, caught between worlds, a little dizzy. He tried to bring her back, but she shoved him off, she gathered her open blouse together. "Oh God," she said. "Who is it?" She scrambled to her feet. When Arnie stood up he saw the figures behind the little hillock. "You bastards!" she screamed, running at them, kicking sand, picking up handfuls of sand and throwing it toward them. They were all there, the four of them, and they were all laughing.

She never even turned back or said anything. She ran for the house. He got himself together and started after her. They were all sprawled in the sand, just laughing. "Hey man!" said Arthur.

Arnie tried to get to her but she was already in her car. She started the motor. She was crazy. She backed up and hit the fender of Red's Renault. She drove forward and backed up and rammed it again. She knocked over the cycle and then zoomed down the drive.

26

A Very Significant Death

ARNIE SAT ON THE BEACH for a long while before he went back. The house was dark. The only light came from the fireplace in the den, the orange light illuminating their faces with an alien glow. Arthur sat crosslegged, the bowl between his knees, a little packet of the white stuff and the powdered parsley and the cigarette papers. Barry lay on the rug, his head on a Moroccan pillow, red and black and purple under his fine, rather lifeless hair. Beside his hand was a gold goblet filled with pills and a bottle of wine. His eyes were open. He stared at the pattern of little wood squares that decorated the ceiling. Red curled beside the fire, his hands pressed between his knees. Mathilda lay back against Red's sleeping body, humming to herself softly. Beulah was out of the jar, resting between Arthur's legs, comfortably secure in Arthur's presence. Arnie approached this circle. "I need to go home now," he said.

There was nobody in any condition to take him home. Barry tried to open his eyes, moving himself into a sitting position in slow motion, one vertebra at a time, as if space itself were thick and he had to push against it. He reached out for a little hand-rolled cigarette that Arthur passed him and held it out to Arnie.

"Why did you do that to Francie and me?" Arnie asked. "Why did you do it?"

Barry smiled his beatific smile. "Be peaceful," he said.

"I thought you were my friend. Why did you hurt Francie and me?"

"Dream," said Barry. Barry lay back to his own dreams.

There was no place for him to go. He never had alternatives. His life was a small closed room with only one or two doors. What was put on him in those rooms, he was stuck with. Because they were the rooms where Arnie lived. He reached into his back pocket for his Hohner. The pocket was flat.

For a split second he experienced total terror, a sense of loss as deep as space. He had no voice! He was in a dark place without a voice! Help! He wanted to call for Amy to come and get him out!

"Arthur . . ." But Arthur was busy rolling the little cigarettes. He put a little pinch of the stuff on the floor in front of Beulah. "This is your party too, baby." Beulah waited for any other signals, then she moved lightly and easily across the floor in her high-stepping walk to the edge of the stuff. She waved a leg in the air. She touched the edge of it. Some white powder stuck to her lovely dark coat. She stood poised like that. And then slowly she backed away.

Arthur handed a cigarette to Arnie. "It's okay, man. We're here with you."

Arnie wanted another door. His heart was stuffed with anger that there was no exit. He couldn't cry. There was nothing he could ask because he didn't know what he needed exactly. Except to go to Francie and he couldn't get there. The questions in the room were too profound. They crackled in the fire, they popped in the logs. Outside through the glass walls he could see the moon on the sea. He thought of himself and Francie on the sand, of what had happened. He didn't know what to do. He never knew what to do. Nerd! Nerd! He wanted to comfort Francie but there was no way to reach her. So he took the cigarette and let Barry lean over with his gold lighter to light it and he leaned back and smoked.

*

When he opened his eyes again he saw Mars Fletcher, the tall familiar angular body of Mars, with someone extremely beautiful dressed in black. A golden woman in a black dress. Mars stood over the sleeping Barry. "Doesn't it make you want to puke?" said Mars.

Barry's eyes opened in alarm, but he seemed frozen, his body unable to respond. But his eyes responded. Maybe Mars didn't see it but Arnie did. They rested on Mars, those hungry eyes, in a kind of tender love seen in the eyes of young calves.

The golden woman was hanging onto Mars's arm. "I couldn't handle it," she said to Mars. "Don't ask it of me," she said. "I simply couldn't."

"He's going back to Tucson with his mother," said Mars.

Barry tried to sit up but he couldn't. He was caught in a fog, sitting at the end of a long tunnel, trying to get to his father, but space was thick and the air was thick and sounds echoed hollowly. Mars Fletcher waved the golden woman in black away from him. She walked off through the patio doors and stood in the garden looking out at the sea.

Mars looked down at Barry and then squatted beside him, rocking on his heels. "Barry, I'm sorry," he said. He moved back and forth on his heels, in some kind of prayer or incantation. "I tried," he said finally. "I can't handle it anymore either. When you were younger . . ." He touched Barry's arm, and then let go. "When you were little it was easier. Now I just can't stomach it. You're the only thing I've failed at in my life."

Arnie blinked his eyes. Time must have passed, because Mars Fletcher was no longer there, nor the woman in black. Maybe they were never there. Maybe it was a dream.

Arthur sat swinging his arms in a kind of dance. Beulah, on good behavior, sat nearby nibbling something with her little mandibles, holding the little tidbit between her two paws. Mathilda's eyes were starkly open but she didn't speak. Red was snoring. His pants were wet. He had wet himself.

Barry wasn't there.

Arnie heard somebody crying. He thought he did. He tried to turn his head but space was still slow. It took him a long while to get up and move. It sounded as if a little child were crying in a room a long way off, in some farther place, like being in a hotel and hearing some child crying someplace down the hall because its parents had gone away and left it in the empty night.

"What's that, man?" asked Arthur.

"I don't know," said Arnie.

Arthur checked to see that Beulah was safely in her place and with a gargantuan effort he picked himself up.

Barry was curled on a big leather sofa, crying, his eyes closed, his legs pulled under him, his head cradled in his arms like a little kid, crying out his heart.

Arthur staggered over to the chair and leaned over him. "Hey man. Don't, man. Hey man, I love you, man. Don't be hurt like that." He tried to touch Barry, to stroke his arm. Barry's eyes opened, like a mechanical doll that had suddenly been set in motion. His hands were trembling. "Man," said Arthur in deep sympathy, "come on, I understand, man. I know how it is. It's okay."

Barry looked up with such hatred, he recoiled, he looked at his hands wet with his tears, at the pillow he held, at Arthur bending over him. His Fletcher eyes turned hard, inward with schemes and plans, inward to the biggest empty space in the world. He shoved Arthur's arm aside and ducked out under it.

"Ain't nothing to be ashamed! Come on, man . . ."

Barry stalked the room like a crazy man, looking down at Mathilda, at Red, at the empty caviar jars, the Poland Water, the bottles of English Rye, the broken glasses, the wet spots on the Persian rug. Then at Beulah. Beulah.

Nobody else was moving fast. He walked over to the bookcase and lifted the big unabridged dictionary from its stand. He lifted it with the kind of herculean strength hypnotized people have. He walked over to Beulah, where she waited obediently for Arthur to return and put her in her jar for the night. Maybe it was past her bedtime. She had been up for a long time, like a kid who isn't used to party hours. Anyhow she didn't move. Barry lifted the dictionary over her. Arthur screamed once, a high-pitched scream. Mathilda and Red both woke up. Red's face flushed in horror. Mathilda gasped. Before they could really focus or understand, Barry dropped the dictionary.

It fell flat. What Arnie heard was a giant *pop*. Like a round globe of a sea plant, the rubbery water-filled kind, when you step on it at the beach. *Pop*.

All you could see was this little tip of black that showed against the beige carpet under the edge of the book.

Arnie saw all this through a kind of anesthetic haze. All he remembered before falling asleep again was Arthur hitting Barry with the fireplace poker.

That was it.

27

What Light from
Yonder Window Breaks

RED DROVE ALONG the Pacific Coast Highway. There was
almost no traffic, the lights were all out in the little beach
houses, and only the moon exposed the sea. Mathilda was
quietly crying. Red drove erratically, his eye was twitching
and he kept rubbing it. "I'm going to have to throw up," he
said to Arnie. But he didn't and kept driving. "I'll drop you
off at Francie's but I can't wait. I'm feeling really ill."

Francie's house was a huge walled estate north of the highway, on the cliffs overlooking the sea. A lot of the land had
crumbled out from under the grounds in the last slides and the
terraces looked perilously undermined. They drove up the side
street that led to the entrance, but the gate was locked. "So
what do you want to do?" asked Red.

Arnie got out.

"Can you get home okay?"

"Sure."

Once he was out, Mathilda slumped down in the whole
back seat and kept on crying. Arnie slammed the door and
Red drove away.

A stone wall surrounded the house but a tall eucalyptus grew within striking distance. He climbed the tree and put a leg over the wall and fell on the other side, tearing the knee out of his pants. The place looked like an old Southern mansion with a wide porch and heavy columns. He could hear music. They must have been having a party inside. The long circular drive was jammed with cars. He headed toward the house, circling around back of it, hoping he could find which room was hers.

The dogs must have leaped out when they heard his steps. They came flying toward him, two Dobermans, muzzles forward, jaws open. He stopped absolutely still. He wasn't even afraid. All he was afraid of was that he wouldn't find her, that she was hurting someplace and not with him. The dogs were confused by his passivity. They skidded to a stop and stood snarling at him, dripping saliva. He reached out a hand. The dogs waited, trying to figure it out. He liked dogs, actually. He could see no dog that he could consider an enemy. Words were enemies. People. Situations. Not animals who belonged to the same general category as himself. Finally the dogs relaxed their tails and ears and came lumbering over, sniffing him. He squatted and took one about the neck and put his face down to it. The dogs licked him.

Then he started out again with the dogs as companions.

He could see her if he stood far enough back. Her room was on the second story, off a shallow balcony. Her curtains were open. He could see her clearly, sitting in front of a mirror staring at herself. Just staring at herself. If he could understand nothing of the rest of the world, he understood how she felt. He could read her heart. If he had had the Hohner, he could have played out the way she felt. He needed to talk with her. "Francie!" She probably couldn't hear him because of the music. The amplified jazz combo blasted into the night. He tried to find some pebbles to throw at her window. But the dogs thought he was trying to play with them and they began to leap in excitement. One of them brought a small twig for him to throw.

He figured that he could climb the heavy bougainvillea that grew thickly at the corner of the house. He tested his weight on the woody vine. The thorns were sharp. They cut through his pants and scratched his leg. He had to get to her. He moved slowly up, trying to avoid as many of the thorns as possible. Below the dogs sat and waited, interested.

He managed to get a leg over the balcony. "Francie!"

She was wearing some sort of feathery gown, probably her mother's. And her hair was semi-piled on her head and tied with a red scarf. She had been crying, he could see that. Her face was streaked with mascara. She was staring at herself in the mirror, putting on fresh lipstick. She must have seen him in the mirror behind her. "What do you think you're doing?"

He pulled the other leg over the balcony. He didn't know what he was doing, except that he knew he had to help her, or say something to wipe away the terrible thing they had done to her, to them both.

Her face twisted in that old sarcastic grimace. "What do you think you are, some kind of Romeo? You poor sap."

"I want to talk to you." He didn't know what he was going to say.

"You're bleeding all over the place. You look like you've been crucified."

He didn't feel the scratches. He knew that something was expected of him. To hold her. To comfort her. To bring her solace. To protect her from the world, because they were two aliens living on the wrong planet. He wanted her to wait by the rock, with Egan, while he went to explore the possibilities of living on that other planet. He wanted to take her there. "It isn't any use," she said. "None of it. No matter what you do, they've got you."

"I want the sheep," he said. "I'll go to Montana and I'll

phone you and you come and meet me and we'll fly to France and buy the sheep."

He put a hand up to her face. Not on it, just near it, so that he could feel the aura of energy. Beauty was very funny. It was funny that her face should be so beautiful to him. He saw his own nerdy face in the mirror but he tried with all his might not to grin, to make it look more serious, or something.

The music was blaring from downstairs. You could feel the hard loud beat in your stomach.

"They finished shooting," said Francie. "They brought home the whole cast."

He wanted to lock her door, but her door wouldn't lock. He sat on the edge of her bed and held a hand out to her. She came to him like a dreamwalker and sat next to him. Then in the most natural way he put both arms around her. He let his face rest in the warm creases of her throat until she put her arms around him also. They rocked a little, holding each other that way, and then they let themselves fall sideways onto the bed. They lay face to face, warm and loving. Her eyes were so soft. "You dumb idiot," she said, but lovingly, like a caress. "You're an idiot savant and I'm a basket case. Don't you know that?"

"No," he said. "I love you."

They lay together under the stars of the meadow in the south of France. He could almost hear the sheep bleating and the panting of the dog running through the high grasses to keep the sheep from leaving the security of the flock. He could have lain there forever.

Neither of them realized that the door had opened. "Well, will you look at this?" Her mother stood in the open doorway, a drink in hand, looking in. Three or four men stood behind her. All laughing at them. "Would you *believe* this?" her mother said.

Francie was totally flustered. "It's just one of the kids from school!" The old nasal sarcasm had returned to her voice.

"Well, don't kids from school knock and use the front door anymore?"

"Not if the bedroom is closer," said one of the men.

Francie's mother turned on the light. The mad hackeress, as Francie had described her, a beautiful brittle overlifted face, and all the robot men behind her bland, handsome, and empty. Her mother seemed more amused than upset. "Well, Francie, is this some little tryst you've arranged?" She bent to see who was occupying Francie's bed. As she looked at his face her eyebrows arched. Her lips curled into an amused sneer. "What do you think you're doing?" she asked Arnie.

He didn't know how to explain it. "I don't know," he said.

"He doesn't *know!*" laughed one of the men. "Should I explain it?"

Francie's mother took a sip of her drink and gave Francie a snide little smile. "Couldn't you do any better than this?"

Francie was dazed by the light. She threw up an arm against it. But it was the klieg light. The scene was being shot. The whole cast was watching her, waiting for her lines. He saw in her face what she felt. He saw it all. When she looked at her mother's beautiful face, and all the faces of the men, men who kissed her mother's hands and took her to restaurants in Beverly Hills and pulled chairs out for her and took her to the south of France to make love to her. It wasn't anger Arnie saw on Francie's face. It was longing and love and hopelessness. "Are you *kidding?*" Francie said, with that old sarcasm. "This is just some nerd from school. He's been after me." She made a stagy face. "You know how irresistible I am." She cast a depreciatory glance at Arnie. But turned toward him, away from her mother, her face told him two separate things. Her mouth said one thing. But her eyes on him said something else. And he understood.

"Toss him," said her mother.

They grabbed him by the back of the pants and by the shirt. His shirt tore. They hefted him by his belt and dragged him down the hallway and down the stairs. They dragged him out the front door and threw him down the steps.

"Easy!" called Francie's mother. "I don't need another lawsuit."

He lay there until his head stopped spinning. The dogs came over whimpering, nuzzling him. He looked up at the house. They were all standing in the doorway watching him, the men laughing, Francie behind her mother, close to her mother, holding on to her mother's arm.

28

Cry Havoc

ALL THE LIGHTS in the house must have been on. It was the only lighted house on the block. Arnie tried to make it up to his room but the study door was open. He heard his mother scream his name. She came at him arms outstretched, those heavy unhappy eyes fastened on him. "He had an accident! God, I knew it! His face is bleeding!"

They all rushed out. "Oh for Pete's sake!" said Hal. "That's not blood, that's lipstick! I told you where he was!"

Amy pushed through to him. "He is hurt! Look at his legs! Oh Arnie, what have you done?"

"What on earth happened to you?" asked his father.

"He cannot take care of himself," said Miriam. "You see."

"Son, what happened?"

"Nothing happened."

"You have your answer," said Miriam.

Tante Hannah stood on the edge of the circle, her arms crossed, saying nothing.

"He was out with the bums, I told you. Everybody in town

probably saw him. Ask him if he's in trouble with the cops. I warned him."

Tante Hannah put out her hand and moved them aside. "Would you like to talk with me?" she asked him.

He said no. He only wanted to get into a hot tub.

"I'll run the tub for you," said his mother solicitously. "Do you need a doctor?"

"I'll run it myself," he said.

While the water was filling the tub, she stood with a towel in her hand. "Everybody else's children," she said. "I have advice for everybody else's children, and I've failed my own. Why?"

Every other time he said, "You didn't." This time he didn't answer.

He got into the tub and soaked. His mother stood outside the door and asked him every two minutes if he was all right. He couldn't work it all out. Not without the Hohner. And that was gone. He went sick to the stomach to think of it there in the sand, sand drying out the heart of it.

He was already in bed with the lights out when he remembered Francie's basement and all the guns. He sat bolt upright. He ran down the hall to the study. He stood with the phone in his hand. He didn't know how to reach her. He didn't know if they had Directory Assistance in the middle of the night. She would be unlisted. He could call Mathilda. But he didn't know how to spell Mattheissen, and Mathilda's mother might be there. He replaced the phone. No, there was nothing he could do.

He lay awake for a long while until the blackness of sleep came.

29

The Sound of Silence

HE LAY LISTLESSLY on the top of the covers with the window open. A hummingbird hovered over a small blossom on a branch of the bottlebrush outside his window. He wanted to be joined with the fluttering of those wings, or with the wind, or with the rhythm of the earth itself. To have to interact with anything human and personal was intolerable.

A number of people knocked. He didn't answer. Finally his father demanded an answer, to know if he was all right, or else the door would be forced. He said he was tired and could he please sleep. His father went away. Amy came by and asked if he wanted to play checkers. He didn't answer. Once he heard a sharp smack on the door, one quick bang. He knew it was Hal. Arabelle said she was leaving a tray outside with her good black bean soup and fresh French bread. When she came back a half-hour later and found it uneaten, she demanded to be let in. So he let her in. She stood by the side of the bed until he finished it. Once he heard his mother crying outside his door. Then they all left the house and it was silent. So he slept away most of the day.

It must have been late afternoon when Tante Hannah knocked. "May I come in?"

He got up and opened the door but went back to bed.

"I didn't hear any music," she said. "I wondered why."

He turned away from her. "I lost my harp."

He heard the scraping as she pulled a chair to the side of the bed. "Why do you call it a harp?"

"Because that's what they call it."

"Who are *they?*"

"Nobody. People who play it."

"People."

"Guys. Guys who play it."

"Why a *harp* particularly?"

"I don't know why."

"Aren't you curious? Since it's an instrument you play?"

"No," he said.

She thought about it. "There's a little mouth instrument called a Jew's harp. Perhaps that's why."

"They just call it that."

"They. You mean a category of people who play the instrument."

"I guess."

"And you belong to that category."

"I don't know," he said.

"Oh yes you know."

He said, "I don't."

"You're very angry," she said.

"I'm not."

"Are you sure?" she said.

"I'm just tired."

"Shall I buy you a new harp?"

"I don't know. Okay, if you want."

"What particular kind?"

"A Hohner."

"But what kind of a Hohner? Is there a different instrument for amateurs and for professionals?" •

"I don't know."

"Yes I think you know since it's a category you belong to. You are a harp-player. That's what you do, Arnie. And you do it well. You know that, don't you."

"I don't belong to anything."

"So you say," said Hannah. "It's part of the game you play."

"I don't play any *game*," he said. He fell silent. In that cushion of silence, he could hear the buzzing of a plane. Maybe it was going to the south of France. "If Marshall played the flute," he said, "they'd nip it in the bud."

He heard a snort of a laugh. "Did Miriam say that?"

"You can't make a living from a flute."

"My sister is a joke. Did you ever hear of Jean-Pierre Rampal? He makes a living with a flute. And your cousin Marshall is completely tone-deaf. He couldn't play a player piano. And why do you believe Tante Miriam when you don't believe me?"

"It doesn't matter," he said.

"Doesn't it, Arnie?"

When he didn't answer, she went away.

He stayed in his room all day Sunday, watching TV. Nonstop. Everything. He heard a religious revivalist say that Los Angeles was going to split away from the coast and sink into the sea because Hollywood was such a place of sin. He saw a Japanese movie about a monster who shot rays into the Empire State Building. He watched a nature program, but he was afraid they might show spiders so he turned to cartoons instead. He only opened the door for Arabelle's trays. She made black-mushroom pizza and chocolate malts with Häagen-Dazs ice cream. He watched *Sixty Minutes* but they had a story about a guy who sold guns. He said selling guns was just a business like any other business. He sold them to both sides of a war that was going on. The only people he wouldn't sell to were enemies of the United States. He smiled when he said it. Arnie wanted to talk to Francie about it but she wasn't there. When he thought of her, his stomach hurt.

On his dinner tray, he found the new Hohner. He put it in a drawer without taking it out of the box.

Late in the evening, his mother knocked and asked, "Why must you hurt me like this?"

He said, "I'm sorry," through the door.

He didn't sleep much.

After the house settled into silence, he listened to the night sounds: a hooting dog, a child crying someplace. Or it probably was just a bird. A bird that sounded like a child crying. He heard that sound for a long while.

30

Old Soldiers

HE AWOKE to Arabelle's knock. He opened the door to let her in. She handed him a freshly ironed shirt and clean pants. "They are all downstairs waiting for you."

"I'm late for school," he said.

She handed him a small religious figurine, a little carved ivory Mary with a tear rolling down her cheek for the dead Jesus, her lost son. "Put this in your pocket. I am praying for you."

"This is your best Mary."

"If they do this thing," she said, "I am leaving this house."

He dressed. He put the figure in his shirt pocket. He smoothed down his hat and folded it and put it in the usual back pocket. He reached for the Hohner, which went into that pocket with the hat. He tried not to remember why it wasn't there. The new harp was in the drawer. He couldn't think about that either. They were all waiting downstairs. He put on his regular shoes and combed his hair. He took his notebook and went down.

They were all sitting around the dining room table waiting for him. Tante Miriam and Hal, his mother and father, Tante Hannah. Not Amy. Amy wasn't there. He needed Amy. He waited to see if she was coming. But she wasn't there.

His mother looked upset and anxious. "This is a mistake," she said. Tante Miriam touched her hand with those long-nailed fingers to quiet her. Hannah watched it and said nothing.

Between Hal and his father was the man, the old soldier. He wore a uniform from some indeterminate war, his chest was full of medals, little colored ribbons, insignia. His hair was iron gray and he wore a clipped gray moustache. Arnie's father started to make introductions, but the old soldier rose, holding his father back. He put down his napkin. He walked over to where Arnie stood. He held out his heavy club of a hand. "I am Major Everts. And you are Arnold Schlatter." Arnie accepted the hand. The major squeezed it hard, a manly handshake. The major waited. Arnie didn't know for what. Then the major took the notebook from under his arm and placed it on the sideboard. "Like a gentleman," said the major. He led Arnie to the table. "Arnold and I understand each other. We will be good friends. Gentlemen and friends."

Arnie sat. Something was expected of him. He didn't know what. Hal poked him. He didn't know what for.

Arabelle came in and placed a plate of food in front of him, looked daggers around the table, and left. He sat there dazed and waiting. Tante Hannah had a cup of coffee in front of her. She wasn't drinking.

"The mind," began Major Everts, talking to the table as if he were giving a lecture, "the mind can become flabby as the muscles can. And if you're a bunch of flab, what do you do?"

Amy ran into the room, she saw Arnie, she saw the major, she started to cry and ran out again.

"You were saying," said Tante Miriam, bringing them back.

"That when the muscles are flabby, you exercise. You run,

you push yourself. You lift weights until it hurts. But in the end you get your reward."

"Why does it have to be pain?" his mother asked in alarm.

"Please," said his father annoyed, "just listen."

"The mind is flabby and asleep. We jog the mind, Arnold. We jog it, we run it, we climb it up high hills."

"Son," his father explained, "what he's saying is that you haven't reached your potential. That you have more ability than you've used."

"Miracles," said Tante Miriam. "I've seen it with others. Just ask my friends."

Tante Hannah sat with her hands over her coffee cup like a fortuneteller divining over a crystal ball but she said nothing.

"But you have to want it, son! Now your father will insist, and you will come, of course. But if you want it yourself! If you say, Major, I'm ready! Major, I will! Major, I can! Say that, son, and I guarantee you twenty points! No, thirty! You can return to your mother and your father proud, a different man! Make the stand yourself! What do you say!"

They all waited for what he had to say.

Hal nudged him, waited, and nudged again.

"I don't care," said Arnie.

The major was totally shocked. "You don't *care!*" The major's face went red with consternation. "You can look at the faces of your concerned parents and have the nerve to say to me that you don't *care?*"

He pushed away from the table and stood up.

"So you see," said Tante Miriam victoriously.

He picked up his notebook and said, "I have to go to school now." He walked out of the house. He looked prayerfully for the Maserati, for Francie sitting there with the windows up singing to the car radio. He needed her. It wasn't there. He felt for the Hohner. It wasn't there. He turned and looked back to the house for Amy. She wasn't there. So he ran.

He ran about a mile. He hitched a ride up to Sunset. He

stopped at a coffee shop in the Palisades for a doughnut and some milk. He tried to eat but he couldn't. When he saw kids begin to walk by, he went along with them.

He walked through the school gate as if it were any other day of his life.

31

Fire and Ice

RED SAT ON A BENCH near the cafeteria, like a mummy, stiff, trying not to move his head, starkly pale, deathly pale. Mathilda sat beside him. She wore a pair of old jeans and a turtleneck sweater. Her hair was brushed back and tied. She wore no makeup. Neither of them spoke. Arnie sat himself on a bench nearby, waiting for Arthur. The kids from the bus walked by, but Arthur wasn't with them. Finally Barry walked over and sat. His eyes were red, the lids swollen. The back of his head was shaved, and there was a bandage over the bare spot. He didn't speak either. He just sat there, cracking his knuckles.

Nobody spoke.

Arnie went back to watching the kids come in. He wanted Francie. He wanted her to wave and call him in her impatient voice and for the Maserati to be there and for them to drive back to the ocean with the speed of light, or to turn into the canyon road. He sat on the edge of his seat expecting it to happen.

Then he saw her. She walked by with a bunch of other

girls, hardly distinguished from them. She wore a blouse and a cotton skirt and her hair was tied up in a kerchief. Her eyes were focused on the ground. He started to go after her, but she slipped into a little knot of people and headed toward the buildings as if she didn't want to talk.

He couldn't believe she wouldn't talk to him. He was stunned by the sense of loss. He didn't know what else to do.

So they all sat like statues while the school day got itself in motion. The first bell rang. They never moved with the first bell. A few people did, and started to form streams of pedestrians headed for class. They just sat and waited, for what he didn't know.

When the little commotion started it wasn't quite evident in all the other movement. Just a few people beginning to run toward the science building, so that you could see a pattern. And others turning to see what was happening and following out of curiosity. Red didn't bother to look up. Neither did Mathilda. Barry's sick eyes were on Mathilda, as if he wanted to say something, but he didn't.

Science building. It came to him like a dream, that something bad was happening to her. Everybody was running now. Now there were voices, telling them to stay back. Now Llewelyn came running from the front office, down the path toward the science building, shoving kids aside, telling them to go back to class.

Arnie was a dreamwalker. This was a dream. All this. He started to move toward the science building. He said, "Francie," in a conversational tone of voice. Nobody heard him.

He heard the ambulance's whine. First from a distance, and then coming closer. Nearer the campus. He started to run. There was a crowd gathered outside the door to the science building. "What happened?" somebody called over the rubbernecking crowd.

He knew what happened! He knew! *"Francie!"* But people were crowded in front of him. Then the ambulance pulled into the quad, over the grass, hitting the siren for space, and parked in front of the science building. The double doors opened. He ducked between people, he pushed people aside. Two men in white ran in with the stretcher. He tried to push forward.

Somebody grabbed his shirt. Hal was behind him. "Stay out of it! Keep out of trouble. Haven't you done enough?"

He tried to push Hal away but Hal kept following him, holding him back by the shirt.

"Why do you have to make a spectacle of yourself! All the time! If you want to make an ass of yourself then go to Montana and do it there! Where we won't have to take it also, okay?"

"Let me go!" He ducked and bobbed to see what was happening. But Hal hung on. Then the crowd hushed. He could see them carrying her out. Her, on the stretcher, an arm thrown up over her face so that she couldn't see them staring at her. Her wrists were bandaged, and they were red. With blood. He knew it. He screamed, *"Francie!"*

Hal pulled his arm sharply. "Will you shut up and stay out of it! Just shut up!"

He tried to get to her, Hal hanging on. *"Francie!"*

She must have heard his voice. As they were putting her into the ambulance she lifted her head. She held up her wrists to him. "I didn't even do this right." He tried to push through to where he could speak with her, but they had put her into the ambulance and were closing the doors.

Then the sirens started to blare and she was gone.

It hit him like a tidal wave coming unexpected out of a quiet sea. The roar. It came up out of his mouth. He doubled up both fists. He turned on Hal and came at him punching. He smacked Hal on the side of the face and hit him in the stomach.

The rest of the crowd pushed back and a circle formed. It just opened. Suddenly they were two fighters in a ring. Nobody laughed. He heard somebody say, ". . . his brother." He threw another right and hit Hal on the side of the face.

Hal was stunned. He stood stiff, like a robot, as Arnie wove around him, waving his fists, taunting. "Fight me!" He threw a right and got Hal on the side of the nose. Hal's nose began to bleed. Hal put a hand up to his nose as if he couldn't believe the blood. Arnie came at him again.

Hal jumped back and held up a hand. "Don't!"

"Fight me!" Arnie screamed. "Come on! Fight!" Now he was swinging wild, waiting for counterblows, inviting them, taunting Hal to throw them. But Hal just backed away, held up both hands, palms outward. His nose was bleeding onto his linen shirt, bloodying up his soft English shirt.

"Fight me! Hit me! Fight *me!*"

Suddenly Hal came at him, throwing both arms around Arnie's shoulders, hanging there, like a fighter in a clinch. Arnie tried to break it, but Hal hung on. He couldn't swing. "I can't fight you," Hal said. "I can't. You're my brother, Arnie."

Finally Arnie pulled away and left Hal standing there and ran.

32

Requiem
for a Departed Friend

ARNIE WASHED HIS FACE in the bathroom. A couple of
people came in and looked at him with curiosity but said nothing. He hadn't been hit but his face looked swollen. His head
buzzed. He wasn't sure what he was supposed to do now. The
tardy bell had already rung. He dried his face and he went to
class.

They were already inside, except for Mathilda, who sat on
the ground outside the door, her back against the wall, crying. When she saw Arnie she said, "Is she dead? Did she do
it?"

He couldn't answer. He was empty of everything.

"She always said she would do it. It's my fault. I made her."

Arnie gave her a hand up. She looked so different with her
hair back and a plain sweater and jeans, he could hardly
recognize her. She was more beautiful. Much more. But he
couldn't say that. He couldn't say anything. What was the use
of saying anything. Nobody heard him.

They were already in their seats, in a manner of speaking.

The jocks in various odd places, their feet in the aisle, smirking at the teacher, who looked pretty upset herself. Mrs. Corregian was in the room with her, they bent to confer, Corregian looked around the room shaking her head. Then Corregian said, "I don't know what you expect to accomplish. Once the cake is spoiled, you can't resurrect it."

Mathilda took her seat and put her head down on the desk. Red was in his seat already, his hands folded on the desk, looking pretty awful. Barry's eyes were closed.

Finally Corregian got ready to leave. She stood for a moment in the front of the room, waving a pudgy finger at them. "I warn you," she said, "any more of this nonsense, and you'll get it in the quiche and brownie department. And I mean it." She walked out.

It wasn't just Barry and they who looked exhausted, just played out. It was most of them. They were all tired.

And the teacher was nervous. She stalked around for a while, waiting for an axe to fall, a sword of Damocles, something to happen. She looked at Barry. His face had completely broken out. It was terrible. He looked like a leper. She had to turn away. "Now you all listen to me!" she began.

Red raised his hand. "I want to ask . . ."

"Shut *up!*" she said.

He shut up.

It shocked them all.

She stalked the front of the room, holding herself in tightly, as if if she didn't she might hit somebody. "Friday," she said, "Friday was one of the sad performances of my life. Sad to see what is happening to kids. I came into this class to teach, not to waste your time or mine. I don't know how to get through this shield you all carry around yourselves, and I'm not going to try to figure it out. So I'm simply laying down the rules. I have two stacks of work on my desk. *Two.*"

Mathilda raised a hand.

"No!" she said.

Mathilda looked ashen. "I'm really sick. This time I am."

Mathilda was sick. Sick with something deep. She looked over at Arnie asking him a question. He didn't have any answers for her. But the teacher was watching her. And the teacher said, rather sadly, "I suppose you are. Just give me a chance to finish. I have two sets of work. One is something of value. The other is pure junk. Little papers with little boxes to fill in with check marks. Okay? Now if you want the real work, the thing of value, I will give you my time. And help you. Before school. After school. Call me. I'll give you my number. If you struggle, I'll hold your hand, I won't let you down. If you want that kind of work, you'll have to cross over."

She walked down the center of the room. She began to push chairs aside to make a wide aisle, chairs with big jocks in them. She shoved them and pushed them, violently, until the aisle was a fact.

". . . just cross over and sit on the right side. And welcome. No more funny business. Do you understand me?"

The response was total silence.

"And the rest of you, I can't change the context of your lives, so if you want to play it this way, just stay where you are on the left side. Fill in your blanks. I'll give you paragraphs to copy out of the encyclopedia and I'll give you a token grade and you can pass out of this class and out of this world, if you choose, because that's what most of you are doing. This is a terrible world. Somebody has to make it straight and it's not you, so just stay out of everybody's way and fill in your little blanks. And go home and watch television and any more of what I had Friday and I'll take you by the seat of the pants, no matter what size, and heave you out personally."

"You can't," said Red. "You can't put a hand on anyone."

"Try me," she said.

His protest was mechanical, no passion in it. "You can't

put a hand on me. You can get into serious trouble."

"They told me," she said. "The Godfather. You want your father to put out a contract on a half-time English teacher? I defy you. So what is it going to be?"

It was Barry they looked to.

His hat went up. He snapped his fingers. Everybody on the right side picked up notebooks and moved quickly over and filled in on the left. Barry, his terrible face, his hurt and blurry eyes. "You and everybody else," he said. "You think you're the first? We get this number once every semester."

They sat and waited and she sat and waited. There was nothing else to say.

Then she heard the sound. The little whistle. The small musical bird song, over her head, from the right, from the left. Then it hovered in the room, almost disembodied, coming toward her. Then it came from Arnie himself. Arnie was whistling. He didn't have his Hohner, he played it by mouth. He whistled a tune. Maybe it was the kind of tune the Pied Piper played, calling the rats to jump over the cliff. Rats weren't lemmings. He had looked up *lemmings*. He whistled a tune that had a sort of finale to it, a resolution of the scale. When he was finished, he took off his hat. He laid it on the desk and flattened it out. Carefully he brushed off the lint. Then he got up. He was long-legged and awkward, he never rose with any sort of grace. He was aware of that. But he did it the best way he could. He walked down the aisle with the hat in his hand. He stopped at Arthur's empty desk. He laid the hat on the desk, the way you lay flowers on a grave. Then he smoothed down his hair with the flat of his hand and he walked over to the Right Side.

"You idiot!" screamed Barry. "Come back here!"

Arnie settled into his chair, tucked his feet under it, looked up to the ceiling and whistled something.

"You nerd! You retard! What the hell do you think you're trying to do!"

Barry just went on that way, for about five minutes. The teacher began to pass out papers. The others watched and waited. Then about five others crossed over, four passives and a guy from the basketball team.

Barry screamed and screamed but nobody was listening. Red kept his seat, but he took off his hat and casually put it on his desk. He cleaned off the derby with the back of his sleeve and then, as if accidentally, looking the other way, he shoved the derby onto the floor.

She passed out the remaining questions and the little easy pamphlets. They looked at the question sheets and the squares to check off *yes* or *no* answers.

To the ones who crossed over she read a story. Arnie closed his eyes and listened. It was a story by Hemingway called "A Clean Well Lighted Place," about a man who was old and afraid of the dark and he went every night to a *bodega*, which was a bar, and stayed there because it was well lighted, and he had no other place to go.

Arnie listened with closed eyes. In the closed-eye place of his mind Tante Hannah said, *You know what she means.* He said, *No I don't.* And she said, *You know more than you let on, Arnie.* He let himself drift to the hospital where Francie lay in pain. He tried to remember when he had last cut himself, how that pain felt, and his wrists hurt to think about her.

When he surfaced, he looked over to the other side of the room, where the disenfranchised sat alone and lonely, the jocks looking out of windows at the colors of the sky. Red had his head down on his desk. Barry sat looking into space, into the vast deserts of Arizona, at the dry sands, and the lizards, and the spiders.

Then the teacher passed blank paper and pencils and asked them to write something. It didn't matter what. Something that was on their mind. Don't worry about form. Or commas. Or anything but feelings. They bent over the papers as if in church. He held the pencil in his hand and wondered what to do.

After a while he wrote out a shaky staff, and tried to work out the sounds of the notes he put down there. He figured that she would know what he was doing.

She had brought Mathilda up to the front of the room. She held Mathilda's hand and let her cry.

33

The Return
of the Whistler

TANTE MIRIAM WAS NURSING Hal, with an ice bag to his
swollen cheek. Hal's white shirt was spattered brown with
blood. Amy curled in the big chair, her feet tucked under, her
face buried in her arms. His father and mother sat like stick
figures, just not knowing how to handle things. They looked
to him. Arnie didn't know how either. He tried Hannah. Hannah sat on a great pillow on the floor in the front of the fireplace, doing needlepoint. She gave him no message. His heart
was turbulent. Should he run? Should he cry? What? He was
just here. The only message he got was something behind him
kicking his butt and calling *nerd, nerd, nerd*.

Miriam shook out a finger at him before she could scrape
words together. "Is this the way to treat a brother?" she said
finally.

Hannah said, "Shut up, Miriam."

"I will not shut up! I have seen enough dillydallying. You
are talking this thing to death." She accused her brother. His
father lowered his eyes. It was one rotten mess-up.

"You have two sons!" said Miriam. "Harold cares about this family. Does Arnie care? Making a public spectacle? At least let the family have some peace." She turned on Arnie. "They have been letting you get away with murder. You are your brother's keeper. Do you understand what that means? If you don't contribute, don't hinder."

"Shut up, Tante Miriam," said Hal. "Just shut up." Miriam fell back, wounded, her little painted doll's fingers fluttering at her heart.

"It's not his fault," said Hal. "He's a nerd. Nerds don't know any better. So lay off him."

"You're a horse's ass," said Arnie.

The room rocked with silence. Hal's mouth sagged a little. Then his face flushed with anger. "And you're a fuckup!"

"You're a pukey jock," said Arnie. "You have as much personality as a stale banana."

"Oh don't," begged Amy. "Don't, please don't, oh don't!"

"Did you hear him?" Miriam sputtered. "Did you hear?"

Whirlwinds swept around his heart. His eyes saw blood. Dried blood on Hal's shirt, blood on the bandages on Francie's wrists, blood on Barry's head. And the little black tip of Beulah under the book. He wanted to play it for them all to understand. He wanted to play how he felt about Hal. But he had nothing to play. He needed a voice. Hannah stood with her eyes bright like the little black bright eyes of a raven, her hands clasped, waiting for his voice. But he had no voice. He searched for a sound to make. He tugged at his stupid hair, at the face that betrayed him in every mirror. Everyone waited. It was for him to say it. *Say what?* He opened his mouth, his voice was scratchy, like an instrument that had been unused too long. "I live here," was what he said. "I live in this house. This is my house too."

His father held a hand out helplessly. His mother started to cry.

For a brief moment, Amy looked happy. Then uncertainty

clouded her eyes, as if she didn't understand his face.

"It's not his house. I live here too."

"How did you think you did not?" wept his mother. "What did I do?"

He left them and started toward his room. The stairs, these were his too. The handrail was his handrail. He climbed the steps two at a time. When he turned, they were all standing below. His father looking up at him, bewildered, trying to find an answer to give him. "I won't go," he said again. "I live *here*."

His father climbed the steps after him slowly, like an old man. When he reached Arnie, he put an arm around Arnie's shoulder. Arnie half-supported him to the room.

He lay on his bed without his Hohner, feeling panic, like a bird floating on thermals, suddenly losing its ability to fly, wondering where it would fall, how hard.

His father walked around the room, trying to relate to it. Looking at the clown fish and the angels which darted around the tank, turning over his rocks, measuring their value, dropping them finally. Picking up and looking at the labels on his records. The old tattered paper cover of *Rollercoaster,* and *Flying Saucer* by Little Walter, his prize. His father couldn't fathom it. "I had a kazoo when I was a kid, but when you grow up, you have to put away your toys." His father set the record down. Arnie lay quietly on the covers, his head on his pillow, touching the soft nap of his blanket, waiting.

Finally his father sat heavily on the edge of the bed. "I'm only trying to do what's best."

"I won't go," he said.

"I'm trying to help you."

"I know."

"If you don't like Silver Hills, then the school your mother chose for you. Learn to play a real instrument, if that's what you want. Learn to read music. Will you give it a chance?"

"No."

"Then what do you want? Where are you going? How will you survive?"

Arnie said, "I don't know."

Where was he going? He thought of the chair on Morris's stage. He thought of Francie lying on the sand. And on the bed. He was so hungry for that. He had come so close. Now Francie lay on a hospital bed alone with the crooks and the spooks, thinking of eyes on flounders and guns in basements. And when she would fall asleep, she would dream of headless fathers. He wanted to see her. He wished he had a dog, a dog without a tail. He would call that dog This Rock Egan. He would not let Hal touch the dog. In fact this dog would follow him and sleep under his bed and when Hal tried to pat this dog, the dog would snarl.

"What am I supposed to do?" asked his father, as if he knew.

He shrugged.

His father rubbed the knuckles of his hand for a while, the way he always did when he lost a case. "Well, I suppose we could get Mr. Schecter in for a few extra hours. Would that help?"

He wasn't thinking about Mr. Schecter. He was thinking about lobsters. How lobsters made it. All that clicking. He had almost made it. He.

Finally his father left.

He was hungry. He wanted to go downstairs and let Arabelle fix him something to eat. But he was afraid to leave his room.

He fell asleep without changing.

He dreamed he could talk to animals.

He opened his eyes when Tante Hannah knocked and called his name.

34

Visit to a Sick Friend

ARABELLE HAD MADE HIM WEAR his English suit, since it was a hospital. But she didn't have any faith in hospital food, which was not fit for humans. So she packed him a paper sack lunch, a couple of her fresh-baked crescent rolls filled with double-whipped cream cheese and lox and she dropped in a handful of the chocolate Turtles which he loved. With bag in hand, he entered the lobby of St. John's.

The waiting room was very crowded. He was too early to visit her ward. So he sat with the others, crying children and nervous parents and a lot of people who were talking about a particular movie star who was upstairs having a heart attack. A few people carried autograph books, just in case.

He watched the creeping hand of the wall clock. Finally it was time. He followed the receptionist's directions to the *Psychiatric Ward, Juvenile*. The nurse who opened the door for him was not uniformed. Neither was the doctor, who wore jeans and a tee shirt, and a beeper in his back pocket. He didn't see anybody who looked particularly crazy. Mostly kids in bathrobes and slippers strolling up and down the corridor. The walls were decorated with their drawings. Angry pictures. Wars. Explosions. Faces of angry gods peering through clouds. In the small lounge, a boy without shoes played a guitar. A couple of girls in bathrobes were watching *The Dating Game* on the TV.

The rooms were off the long corridor. He figured she was in her room. At one of the open doorways he saw a small audience gathered. It was her room. He heard her voice.

The doctor, who ambled over to join the audience, smiled as he listened in. Francie was holding court on her bed, a couple of pillows behind her. She wore one of her mother's silk gowns, pale blue with a little fringe of white feathers around the neck and at the bottom. But her face was clean of makeup and her hair was brushed neatly back and tied. Her bare feet stuck out. She had little pudgy feet. She looked like somebody's kid sister dressing up. Both her wrists were bandaged. Like white bracelets. Like a decoration for her costume. ". . . So I had this breakdown," she was explaining. "I mean it was a three-million-dollar production. When the director found out, he almost committed suicide himself." She waved her hand to explain this. All the little feathers at her throat fluttered. "I mean, who can stand the pressure of all those retakes, day after day. And he kept pushing me. *Francie, you have more to give!* I gave everything I had! I mean, they're like Dracula! Then one night, snap! They found me in the hotel bathtub practically out of blood. Everybody in the cast rushed to give me transfusions. If I told you whose blood is in me right now, you wouldn't believe me."

"Was it a movie for TV?" asked one of the listening girls.

"Are you kidding? I only *do* features."

The girl scratched a rather raw spot on her arm. "I watch *The Edge of Night.*"

"You know Charles Bronson?" asked one of the boys. He was a tall thin boy with a tattoo etched into his upper arm. A dagger slicing a heart and blood dripping. "Could you get him to come here sometime?"

"I slept with him once," confided Francie. "He's not so tough. He's actually gentle when you get to know him."

The girl who was scratching her arm said, "Sometimes I watch *Dallas,* but it gets me too upset."

Then she saw Arnie. She tightened up. She pulled her feathered robe around her.

He said, "Hi."

Everybody turned to see who he was.

"One of the studio musicians," Francie explained. "The whole company practically went into mourning when it happened."

He had broken up the monologue. The show was over. They all drifted back toward the lounge. Except the doctor, who asked him what was in the paper bag.

Now that Francie wasn't animated, she looked pale. She leaned without energy against her pillow. "They're afraid you'll bring in a razor or something. I don't even get a knife in this place. I have to eat with my fingers."

"Come on, Francie," said the doctor. "Be fair."

Arnie opened the bag and offered it to be sniffed. "It's only lox and cream cheese sandwiches. My maid used the Norwegian lox. It doesn't smell as strong."

"That's fine," said the doctor. "We'll send in some milk. How would that be?"

When they were alone, he kicked aside the door stop. "Is it okay to close the door?"

She held herself and rocked on the bed, up and back, inward and private. "You think that doctor is so sharp? All he wants to hear is lurid details of my sex life. I practically memorized Krafft-Ebing. I give him all these juicy details. If he was all that good, he'd recognize them."

He opened the bag and spread two napkins on the bed. "I also brought chocolate Turtles, the kind with walnuts." He unwrapped the foil of her sandwich and handed it to her. The cream cheese had oozed out all around. She took the sandwich and licked around the edges to tidy it up. "My hands hurt. I should have used broken glass instead of that stupid dull lab knife. I really butchered myself."

He licked at the cheese of his own sandwich. "You ought to talk to my Tante Hannah. She's a shrink and you don't have to talk about sex unless you want."

She supported the hand that was holding the sandwich with her other hand. "I've probably shot my whole career. I was thinking of taking up space biology or something like that. Maybe I'll volunteer for a space shot. After what I went through with my mother on this one, I'd rather take my chances with the aliens." She stopped. He could see by her face how much her wrists hurt. "So why did you come?"

"I don't know," he said. "I wanted to see you."

"After what I did? *God,* I can't believe what I did to you. At the house, I mean."

"It's okay. I'm not sore."

It made her angry. "Why? Why are you not sore? You ought to be sore!"

"I guess I understand."

"How come? I mean I'm pretty smart, okay? And I don't understand."

"I know how it is," he said.

"Well, I don't know how it is, not anymore."

He didn't know what to answer, so they both ate the sandwiches. The lox was pleasantly salty and the poppy seeds on the rolls stayed in your teeth. After the sandwich was gone, the alien poppy-seed taste stayed on your tongue. "My Tante Hannah," he said, "she reminds me of you. She tells me stories."

Francie's head was turned toward the window. "They're not going to push lithium on me. I'm messed up enough, okay? I spit out all the pills."

"My Tante Hannah told me this story about a famous shrink named Young."

Now she looked at him. "Not Young, Jung. His name is Jung."

"I thought it was Young."

She sighed her exaggerated sigh. "If he's a famous shrink, it's Jung. Trust me."

He moved closer to her on the bed. "So this lady comes to this doctor and she says, Doctor Young, I have a golden snake in my stomach and sometimes it comes up out of my mouth."

He didn't know if she was listening. She had closed her eyes. She rocked up and back, like someone praying, or someone getting hypnotized.

"So this Doctor Young, he asks her, 'Does it make you unhappy to have a golden snake inside you? Golden snakes are so beautiful.' And she answers, 'No! I love that snake! It's part of me. It makes me happy. It's wonderful!' 'So,' says Doctor Young, 'then why do you come to me?' And she answers, 'When I tell people that I have a golden snake, they say I'm crazy and they want to lock me up. So you'd better help me get rid of the snake.' So this doctor thinks and thinks about it and finally says, 'Lots of people have golden snakes and other beautiful things in them. People who don't understand golden snakes can't see them. And if they hear about a golden snake, they just want to kill it. So this is what I advise you. Don't tell anybody you have one.' And she thanked him and went away happy."

She drew up her knees and kept rocking, like an unhappy kid who doesn't have any other place to move except up and back. "The whole world is full of snake killers. They want that golden snake, boy do they want it. Even if they make you blow off your head to get it. Well I'll really get the nerve one of these days. They'll be satisfied then."

He felt the swelling in his throat. He was choking. "If you

do it, who will I have to talk to then? Then I'll always be alone."

She started to give him a smart answer. But she didn't. Her eyes glazed over. He moved closer now and she let herself be held. "I think I'm dying," she said. "I hurt so bad I can't stand it anymore. I just want to get off their planet."

For a while he rocked with her, trying to think how to say the rest of it. He wanted to take out his new Hohner, and play it, so that she would understand. She was the bird on the sand. The hurt bird. But he was too. He knew that. He felt something for her that was deeper than night, and brighter than the North Star. "If I tell you something, will you laugh?"

She shook her head *no*.

"I dreamed that I lived on an island. All alone, on this island. And one day you sailed there on your father's ship."

Her eyes were open, and hurt, and vulnerable.

"And one day you were walking through the jungles and I saw you."

Someone knocked. The door opened and the nurse came in with two cartons of milk. But she saw them, and ducked her head as if to apologize for intruding and left the milk and closed the door.

"So I followed you," he said. "I stowed away on the ship, in a lifeboat."

She put her arms around him now. "You're crazier than I am. You know that?"

He wanted to get under the covers and hug her but he wasn't going to get away with it.

After a while they divided up the Turtles and opened the cartons of milk and ate them and drank the milk. Then he took out the new harp. It was still stiff. He had to break it in. It wasn't seasoned yet with his breath, and his spit, and the heat of his hands. He couldn't bend the notes just right. He played little tentative circles for a while. Now the nurse opened

162

the door and left it open. A few of the kids drifted back to listen. He was playing something by Poppa Lightfoot, one of the blues stomp classics. A couple of people clapped their hands to the rhythm. The doctor came back to listen and made a little drum out of a table and joined in. Then he played a little early Larry Adler, a blues piece, when Larry was still called Red Pepper Sam. Then he played something special for her.

He knew it made her happy.

He knew how she felt and what she was thinking.

He knew how to make sounds take the shape of golden snakes and white gulls swooping over sapphire waves.

When he finished everybody said he was wonderful and the barefoot boy with the guitar asked him if he wanted to jam the next time he came. He liked that ward. He wished they had a bed for him in her room. He would have slept over.

"He's getting this fabulous record contract," Francie explained. "He'll make a gold record for sure."

He didn't know how to say goodbye with the nurse and all the others standing around. But he figured it was a nuthouse and you could do anything. So he leaned over the bed and kissed her goodbye. She threw her arms around his neck and started to cry.

He played outside under her window for a while. He could see that there were bars on the windows. She pressed against them, listening. They were disguised as something else, but they were bars. He knew bars.

St. John's was only a mile from the beach. He ran all the way. He left his English jacket on the sand for somebody else. He rolled up his shirt-sleeves. For maybe an hour he built himself sand castles, with deep moats around them and high towers. But the tide came in and washed them away. He walked toward Malibu for four or five miles.

Finally, when he couldn't avoid it any longer, he hitched a ride up the hill and went home.